IN MY ENEMY'S HOUSE

OTHER SCHOLASTIC BOOKS
BY CAROL MATAS:

CAROL MATAS

IN MY ENEMY'S HOUSE

cover art by
John Suh

Scholastic Canada Ltd.

Toronto New York London Auckland Sydney
Mexico City New Delhi Hong Kong

To my friend Pnina Zilberman,

with heartfelt thanks

Scholastic Canada Ltd.
175 Hillmount Road, Markham, Ontario, Canada L6C 1Z7

Scholastic Inc.
555 Broadway, New York, NY 10012, USA

Scholastic Australia Pty Limited
PO Box 579, Gosford, NSW 2250, Australia

Scholastic New Zealand Limited
Private Bag 94407, Greenmount, Auckland, New Zealand

Scholastic Ltd.
Villiers House, Clarendon Avenue, Leamington Spa,
Warwickshire CV32 5PR, UK

Canadian Cataloguing in Publication Data

Matas, Carol, 1949–
In my enemy's house

ISBN 0-590-51570-5 (bound)   ISBN 0-439-98829-2 (pbk.)

1. Holocaust, Jewish (1939–1945) — Poland — Juvenile fiction. I. Title.

PS8576.A7994I52 1999   jC813'.54   C99-931285-5
                    PZ7.M423964In 1999

5 4 3 2 1   Printed and bound in Canada   1 2 3 4 / 0

ACKNOWLEDGMENTS

I'd like to thank David Gale, my editor at Simon & Schuster; Diane Kerner, my editor at Scholastic Canada; and Perry Nodelman for their insightful critiques of the manuscript. Thanks also to my husband, Per Brask, who listened and commented chapter by chapter.

Ben Sheletsky told me in detail about his experiences in Poland, and Lea Silberstein described her experiences living with a Nazi family in Germany. I am deeply indebted to both of them. Also my thanks to Sophie Pollack and Kristine Tyndel for sharing the stories of life in Poland, then in Germany. And thanks to Michael Klachefsky, who gave me the tape made by his mother, Natalie Klachefsky, describing her experiences as a Polish worker in Germany.

Many thanks to Pnina Zilberman, who organized my interviews and who read the manuscript for accuracy.

And, of course, to Donna Babcock and Tim Babcock for all the typing and computer work.

Prologue

IF WE KNEW HOW THINGS WERE going to turn out, if we could see the future, would any of us have the courage to live? Would I have had the courage?

It's lucky, isn't it, that we go into the future blind. But the past, that's very different. The past we must look at closely. But sometimes remembering the past is like peering into a kaleidoscope—with each turn you suddenly have a new shape, a new set of colors, a new dimension.

Tomorrow I must go forward. Today I must look at my past. Like the scholar I want to be I must examine it, detail it, understand it. Or try. I have to try.

ONE

"JEWS OUT! JEWS OUT! Jews out! *Raus. Raus. Juden Raus.*"

We could hear their shouts clearly through the open windows in the house. I couldn't move. I couldn't breathe. The Germans had arrived in Zloczow, pushing out the Russians who had occupied this part of Poland for almost two years.

"God protect us," Papa said.

He stood in the kitchen, his long beard and sidelocks quivering slightly as he rocked back and forth, praying. Yehuda looked up from the homework he was doing at the kitchen table. Mama dropped the soup ladle back into the pot and turned to me, the oldest, to help. But all I could do was tremble and shake. Fanny, two years younger than me but so much braver, ran to Moishe who was toddling over to Mama and scooped him up. Sarah hustled into the kitchen from the bedroom and raced over to Fanny who always protected her.

Our door burst open, kicked in by a black boot.

"Jews out. *Raus. Raus.*"

"Children, children, stay with me," Mama called.

I felt dizzy. I swayed a little.

Mama noticed and gave me a sharp look. "Marisa," she hissed, "you are *not* going to faint. Fanny, pinch her."

Fanny pinched me on my arm, hard, so it hurt.

"Ow!" I yelped. But the pain *did* take my mind off the dizziness. The fear, however, grabbed my heart and squeezed and squeezed.

Mother hustled us out into the street. We stood helplessly just outside our door as a German soldier began to scream orders at us, speaking too fast for me to understand. German and Yiddish are very close and I should have been able to follow him but I was too terrified to listen properly, to think straight. I concentrated on one thing—not fainting. I *willed* myself not to faint. We knew from our relatives who lived in places already occupied by the Germans that if I fainted, if I showed any weakness, I might never open my eyes again—I'd probably be shot, right there, on the spot.

"They want our valuables," Mama translated. "They want any money we have, now. Tomorrow we have to get all our jewelry together, our good china, our crystal, our silverware, lamps, carpets, everything. And they say we have to form a Jewish council to collect it all and bring it to them because they are too busy for such work. And all radios must be turned in tomorrow." She paused for a minute as the soldier near us finished shouting his orders. "Yitzhak, go in the house. Get the money that's in the flowerpot. Bring it out."

I knew that most of our money was *not* in the

flowerpot. It was hidden in the basement. Papa nodded his head and hurried back inside. I spotted my friend Sophie across the street with her family. She looked scared, too. Down the street, I could see Reb Shloime with his ten children, the widow Feinschmidt with her seven children, and the Zuckermans at the very end of the block who everyone knew were crazy, all twelve of them, grandparents, parents, and children. Once Chaike Zuckerman bit a dog, right in front of me. And laughed! The poor dog howled all day.

Suddenly the old Mr. Zuckerman and the young Mr. Zuckerman were pushed into the middle of the street. Had they said something? Done something wrong? A German soldier shouted so the whole street could hear.

"Corner house," Mama translated. "He says all men from the corner houses will—"

Before she could finish the German soldier took his pistol out of his holster and shot old Mr. Zuckerman in the head. Then he shot the young Mr. Zuckerman. An all-too-familiar sensation overtook me then, an excruciating dizziness, a feeling of falling so fast that my stomach lurched, and then blackness at the edge of my vision. I hated it but I couldn't stop it—that's all I remembered.

"Wake up, Marisa, wake up." It was my mother. I swam out of the darkness, my head spinning. I'd had some awful dream. . . . "Marisa, they're gone. Wake up. Everyone is safe."

"The Zuckermans?"

"Not the Zuckermans." She shook her head. "We're lucky, I suppose," she continued. "At least they didn't lock us all in the synagogue and burn it down."

I sat up. Mama had put me on the couch. Mama was big and strong and was used to carrying me when I fainted. I took after Papa who was small with fine bones and delicate features, and had a delicate constitution. I was blond like him, too, with blue eyes, whereas Mama and the other children had black hair and brown eyes.

"They are demanding that all the girls report first thing in the morning to clean for them. You and Fanny and Sophie and Chaike and Lotte, you all must go."

I started to shake again. "I can't, Mama. I can't. I'm too scared. What if they shoot me, or decide to hurt us?"

"If you don't go, for sure they'll shoot you," Mama said. Her eyes had a dead look in them and she was calm, as if she weren't talking about her own daughters and their friends.

Papa came over to me, tears in his eyes. "Say your prayers, Marisa. Maybe God will protect you. Your parents can't. Your parents are reduced to *nothing*. What good is a father who can't protect his young?"

He sat down, put his head in his hands, and wept. Papa had wept when little Benjamin died. He had wept for days. That's the only other time I'd seen him cry. He was always so happy. He studied Torah, went to shul, taught, loved his family; he never had a complaint. Even when the Russians occupied Zloczow, he didn't seem to mind. Of course he felt very sorry for the rich Jews who were sent to Siberia. But then he said how lucky for us that God had chosen us to be poor, because the Russians loved the poor. They tried to help us, and somehow we always had enough food. We managed.

"Is God punishing us, Papa?"

"I don't know, Marisa."

"But Papa, if everything is God's will, then this *must* be a punishment."

"Shah, shah," Mama said, "enough of this talk. We have to be practical. We will say our prayers but we will also do what we have to so we can survive. That's how we'll operate from now on. So tomorrow you'll go and clean. I think that's all they want, Marisa, cleaners. The Russians weren't that fussy, you know. But the Germans—everything has to shine. Everything has to be perfect. It was like that when I went to visit Aunt Esther in Berlin. You couldn't find a speck of dust in that entire city."

Mama is probably right, I told myself. The Russians *were* very boorish. And poorer even than we were. The wives of the officers wore felt boots, not even leather, and told us that at home children could go blind from hunger. Imagine. Blind. In Zloczow you might be poor, but you always had enough to eat.

As soon as my head cleared and I didn't feel dizzy anymore I was able to think, and thinking led to worrying. How were my friends? Had anyone else been killed? And how was Shmuel?

Shmuel was the son of Papa's brother's second wife: the son she had *before* she married Papa's brother, Avraham. In other words we were cousins, but we weren't related by blood. If we hadn't been cousins I never would have met him because his family wasn't observant at all. Papa used to say, "They'll cause the Messiah to come early!" (The Messiah will come when the world is in turmoil.) Shmuel was sixteen, a year older than me, tall, with black hair and huge blue eyes. We rarely got a chance to meet, as I couldn't just talk to boys, of course, but at family gatherings we could talk and we did. He was only a baby when his mother remarried so we grew up together. He was the opposite of me. Not afraid of anything! I admired that. But I didn't know whether that would help him or hurt him once the Nazis arrived.

Mama forbade us to go out of doors for the rest of that day and we didn't have a telephone so we didn't know what else was happening. When the war had started two years ago we were afraid that the Germans would take us over but instead the Russians did. We hoped to wait out the war under Russian rule. But when we saw that comet in the sky one dark August night, everyone knew it was a bad omen. So in September of 1941 when the German planes began to bomb Zloczow no one was surprised. The Russians had nothing to fight with; they shot at the planes with pistols and rifles. They didn't even have enough trucks to run away in— they marched out of the city on foot as the Germans advanced. So finally, Germany had conquered almost all of Europe, including us, and they wanted Russia, too. We knew that if they won Russia, there wouldn't be a Jew left alive anywhere.

I didn't tell anyone this but often I thought of different ways to kill myself. After all, if I was going to die anyway, wouldn't it be better to do it in my own way? I'd heard that when the Germans got rid of Jews sometimes they buried them alive because they didn't want to waste the bullets.

I lay on the couch that day and I shook so hard from fear I couldn't stop. Fanny came over and put her arms around me and tried to comfort me. I wished I could be brave like her. Because somehow, the next day, I knew I'd have to go to work for the Germans.

TWO

WE TOOK A STREETCAR into the center of town at six the next morning. We really didn't know what to do or where to go. Fanny walked up to a German soldier and asked where the new head-quarters was. He pointed to the offices that used to house the city clerks. So we went there, arriving at the same time as other girls who obviously had been told to report in for cleaning duty. We stood around awkwardly for a while until a nasty man screamed at us to clean one floor per group. The six of us girls ended up on the third floor.

The soldiers offered us nothing to clean with. Sophie explained to one of the soldiers that we had no cloths or soap with us. She could speak perfect German because her mother was originally from Germany. He told her to clean or else.

What were we to do? We huddled together, me, Fanny, Sophie, Chaike, Adele, Rachel.

"We'll have to use water, we can clean with water," I whispered.

"With our hands?" Sophie objected.

I thought hard and fast. None of us wore a ker-chief—only the older married women had to cover their hair. Our shirts were too short; our skirts were long but not long enough to use as rags. "Our under-pants," I suggested. "That's all we have. We'll have to take off our underpants."

Fanny looked at me, completely shocked. "Marisa, we *can't*! What would Papa say?"

"He'd say do whatever you have to so they don't shoot you," I replied fiercely. "Come. We'll go to the ladies' room, take them off, wet them with water, and no one will know what we're using."

Once we were in the bathroom my friend Sophie started to giggle.

"Quiet," I reprimanded her, looking around nervously.

"There's no one else here," Sophie snorted. "I checked. Wouldn't the Germans just love to know we're cleaning their precious headquarters with our underwear!"

"Mine are very clean!" Fanny protested indignantly.

That made Sophie laugh even harder.

"Maybe," Sophie said, "we should pish on them first, then use them!"

"Sophie," I giggled, "stop it!" But I felt better for laughing. Before I left my house, I'd been so scared I almost *did* pish in my pants. Turning it around like that, even in thought, made me feel stronger as I washed the floors and dusted and worked around the German officers. Fortunately I seemed to be invisible. Every once in a while I stole a glance at them, wondering how it could be that they seemed so normal. Even pleasant. They smiled at one another, went about their work, and yet, some of them had murdered yesterday. Papa had told us when he came home from shul early, before Fanny and I left, that at every corner house a Jew was taken out and shot. Which ones were the murderers? I couldn't tell. A tall fellow with a long, lean face sat at his desk, concentrating hard on some paperwork. A chubby man with pink cheeks and bright blue eyes told a joke and got a few of his fellow workers to laugh. How could they murder a person one day and cheerfully go to work the next? I didn't understand.

I also kept a close watch on Chaike, worried that she might do something crazy to revenge the death of her father and grandfather. But she was silent, working without a glance at the Germans, perhaps still in a state of shock.

At around six o'clock we were allowed to leave and go back to our families. We were told to return the next day. I felt uncomfortable on the long walk home, the wind blowing my skirt, no underwear on. It took us over an hour until we finally reached our street. The first thing I saw was Shmuel waiting on the corner.

We hurried over to him.

Sophie and Fanny started to tease him right away.

"Shmuel," said Sophie, "you must be lost. Can't you find your way home?"

"Sophie," Shmuel said, grinning, "there is such enchantment on this street," and he made a little bow to all of us girls. "How could a fellow *not* get lost?"

He sent a small wink my way. I could feel my cheeks heating up. I knew I was blushing. No matter how anyone tried, I'd never seen Shmuel when he couldn't do one better when he was being teased.

The girls walked ahead while I lagged behind with Shmuel. He towered over me. "Are you all right? They haven't hurt you?"

"I'm fine," I replied. "Scared."

"This time you have reason," Shmuel said. "It isn't like the spiders you used to make me kill, or a wasp or even a shadow at the end of the street. We *should* be afraid." He looked at the pavement. "I don't think we'll make it."

"Shmuel," I said, "that's not like you. Are you giving up?"

He didn't answer directly. "Father had to turn in his radio today. He's lived for the radio, listening day after day to the BBC for news. Now we'll have no way of knowing how things are going in the war. And have you heard, the local Ukrainians have formed a police force and they've started to round up Jews? Apparently this is fine with the Germans— as long as we're gotten rid of, the Germans don't care who does it."

I touched his hand. He looked up and briefly held mine. "I have to get back. Be careful."

"You, too," I said.

I returned home only to see Papa standing on the doorstep.

"Miriam," he said. (He called me that only when I was in trouble; otherwise it was always Marisa, my pet name.) "I will speak to you in my office."

I followed him into the small room he used as a schoolroom.

"Sit down, please," he said.

I sat.

"Miriam, I saw you touching cousin Shmuel out on the street."

"He's not a *real* cousin," I replied, my voice small. My heart was racing. I hated it when Papa was displeased with me. It had happened only a couple of times before. Once I'd been mean to Fanny and he had been very disappointed; once I had spoken rudely to Mama. I always tried to be very good, though, because then Papa gave me his wonderful smile and told me what a blessing I was to him and to everyone.

"This is not about whether or not Shmuel is your cousin," Papa said. "I think I must have been blind. What is going on Miriam?"

"Nothing, Papa!"

"Nothing? Meeting alone with a boy, touching hands, that is nothing?"

"We're cousins!"

"You just denied he is really your cousin!"

"Papa, I'm growing up. I like Shmuel. I like him very much. Don't be mad. I didn't mean to mislead you. But you never say anything nice about him. I knew how you would react."

Papa said, "I can't allow this. He's not right for you. He's barely a Jew."

"He *is* a Jew, Papa. You can be a Communist *and*

a Jew. He belongs to a Zionist group. He wants to go to Palestine."

Papa rolled his eyes. "This is even worse! A bunch of nonbelievers there. Enough. Tomorrow I go to see his father."

"Papa, no!"

He looked at me, then, angry.

"I mean, Papa, *please,* we're doing nothing wrong. I . . . I . . . I've only held his hand this once. Because we were upset. And afraid."

"Once is too many times," Papa declared. "Go help your mother now. I know best."

I don't know what came over me but on my way out I turned and blurted out, "Papa, maybe in this case you don't know best." And I left.

I bit my lip as I helped Mama put the dinner on the table. *How could I speak to Papa like that?* I thought. *He must be terribly upset with me.* All through dinner I wanted to apologize but every time I went to open my mouth I thought of Shmuel and how Papa wanted to keep us apart, and the words wouldn't come out. I could hardly touch my food. Mama told us how she'd spent the day getting ready to hand over all our valuables and when I finally took notice I realized that my favorite little china knick-knacks, our good china lamp, and our cutlery were all piled up neatly in the corner.

"Tomorrow it'll be the carpet," she said, sighing, "and our good china."

"As long as it's only things," Papa remarked. "They can have all our things—if they'll just leave the living, we'll be happy. Things we can replace when this is all over." He looked around the table at us. "You can't replace a human being."

The six of us spent another day cleaning for the Germans, although this time we brought our own rags and a bucket for water. When we got home there was no Shmuel waiting at the corner.

"Marisa got in trouble yesterday," Fanny tattled to the others.

"You're too young to be with a boy," Sophie said, imitating Papa, "and especially *that* boy."

I snapped at Sophie. "My father only wants what's best for me."

"Of course he does," Sophie agreed, surprised at my attack. "I know that."

"I'm sorry, Sophie," I said, "it's just that I feel awful. I spoke back to him. I didn't listen. I'm going to apologize as soon as I see him," I vowed. "Come on, Fanny, let's hurry."

I couldn't get home fast enough once I'd decided what I had to do. With all of Papa's worries, he certainly didn't need to worry about me. Fanny and I rushed into the house only to find Mama at the kitchen table, crying—no, sobbing. The children were crying, too. Then I noticed Shmuel, standing in the corner. His eyes were red; he stared ahead as if he couldn't see me or anything.

"What's happened?" I asked, my voice a whisper, afraid to ask, afraid to hear.

Mama looked up. She shook her head. She

couldn't speak. Yehuda stalked over to me and kicked me sharply in the shins.

"It's *your* fault," he exclaimed. "Papa went to Uncle Avraham's, to talk about you and Shmuel, and while he was there the Ukrainians came, the police, and they arrested Avraham and because Papa was there they arrested him, too."

Fanny let out a small shriek and sank to the ground. I felt dizzy. Shmuel came over and led me to the couch.

I looked at him. "Tell me it isn't true."

"It was just a random thing," he said, his voice faltering. "They targeted our neighborhood for their first raid."

"It's my fault," I cried. "Yehuda is right. If I had listened, if I had obeyed, he wouldn't have had to go to your father. . . . Oh dear God. What will happen to them?"

"They've been put into freight trains," Shmuel said. "I followed them. We don't know. . . ."

"Oh my God, my God," I whispered, "it's my fault. It's my fault. Papa. I'm sorry. I'm sorry. Please come back."

THREE

IT WAS OCTOBER. Fanny and I were walking home from the country. She was carrying a precious sack of flour that we had managed to get in exchange for a bag of our good clothes. It was hot, unusually hot, and I could see thunderclouds to the west.

We still weren't sure what had happened to Papa. The Germans had spent the time since they had arrived separating us Jews from everyone else, although the Poles were also treated terribly. Most of the Polish intellectuals and leaders had been arrested and either killed or shipped off. All schools were closed. Himmler, who was the head of the SS, decreed "A Pole is a slave. It is enough for him to write his name and count up to ten." One of the Nazis we cleaned for had that posted on his desk. Sophie had translated it for us.

We Jews were forced to wear a white armband with a blue star of David on it. It made us so obvious wherever we went; I felt so self-conscious, so vulnerable all the time. Often Jews were pulled off the street to work for the Germans or they were beaten, or shot. They began conducting "actions," mass arrests where they swept through the city arresting hundreds of Jews at a time and transporting them out of the city.

Without Papa it was very difficult to carry on. Mama, who had always seemed to be the strong one, completely fell apart. As the oldest it was up to me to keep the family together, and since it was my fault that Papa was gone—I couldn't allow myself to think that he could be dead—I had to try to keep us going. Also, with my blond hair and blue eyes, when I took my armband off no one could tell I wasn't Polish. And I spoke Polish very well, without any Yiddish accent—after all, I had gone to a Polish public school when we still *had* school.

The food situation was terrible. The shops were practically empty, and of course Jews always had to wait for the Poles to buy first. The farmers had food, though, and prodded by Shmuel to do it, I started going out to the farms, bartering with them. One week I got a sack of potatoes for a sheet. Another time a farmer's wife sold me beets and onions, enough to make soup. But I had to give her the two silver candlesticks Mother had managed to hide from the Germans, for the food. I worried that soon I'd have nothing left to trade and winter was coming.

There had been two "actions" already in our area. Fortunately our neighbor, Mr. Kraszewski, was a Polish military man. When the Russians were in Zloczow, we hid him in our basement, otherwise he certainly would have been arrested. If we heard there might be an action, he hid us in his attic. He was a round, red-faced man, very gruff, hardly spoke a word, but he was a man of honor. I knew he would never give us away. There were Polish neighbors at the end of the street, the Bobrzyrs, who I was not so sure about. Mrs. Bobrzyr spit whenever I walked by and glared at me as if this entire war was my fault. Of course that's what the Nazis had said for years, that we Jews were the cause of the war, and I suppose a lot of people liked to believe it. It made me feel sick inside, but I tried not to think about it. I seemed to spend most of my time trying *not* to think about things.

Fanny insisted on coming with me that day. She was taller than me, and stronger than me, even though she was only thirteen. We were able to carry more between the two of us and the clothes had been heavy—but it was *very* dangerous for her to take off her armband, she looked so Jewish. Every time I went out on the street I was in a state of terror, never knowing what could happen, but that day I was twice as scared, having her along. It was already my fault about Papa. I knew I wouldn't be able to stand it if anything happened to her because I had allowed her to come. But Fanny wasn't like me. She was more like Shmuel. She wanted to fight all of them. I would have hidden under the kitchen table forever if I could.

When we got back to our neighborhood there was an eerie silence all around. The street was empty.

"What's happened?" Fanny asked.

I began to tremble. I knew the signs. In a minute, she realized it, too. An "action." And we were out there, unprotected. We began to run. But not fast enough. We had just reached our house when the Germans arrived in trucks and on foot. They seemed to be everywhere. We couldn't knock on Mr. Kraszewski's door where the others were probably hiding, we'd be seen. So we hurried into our own house.

"The basement," I gasped. "Maybe they won't search the whole house." We ran down into the basement, Fanny still clutching our precious flour. It was only a room with a dirt floor, nothing much in it, nowhere to hide. We cowered in a corner.

I heard the door being slammed open and the sound of boots. More than one pair, at least two. They went from room to room. My heart thudded so hard my chest hurt. I was sweating so much the dirt under my hands began to get wet. Fanny started to say the Shema. I joined her. "'Shema Israel, Adonai Eloheinu, Adonai Ekhad. Hear, O Israel: the Lord our God, the Lord is One.'" We whispered it under our breath, over and over and over until the boots started down the steps and then I couldn't breath well enough to pray. Within seconds they were standing over us, two Gestapo guards, and they began to laugh!

"Here are two little rats!" one declared. I understood the German better by then, having listened to it for two months.

"Rats in the basement," the other agreed, and he

kicked Fanny in the leg, hard. Fanny bit her tongue. She wouldn't scream.

"Oh, a tough little rat," observed the guard who had kicked her. "Try the other one." The second guard kicked me in the side and I screamed, and then I felt faint, but I couldn't let myself faint and leave Fanny alone, so I took a deep breath and tried to stay with her.

The first guard took Fanny's arm and pulled her up. The second screamed at me, *"Raus!"* I scrambled up and grabbed Fanny's hand. They pushed us up the stairs. We were thrown out the door onto the street, and there I saw the widow Feinschmidt. Not all of her children were with her, only the four youngest. The others must have managed to hide. I saw three of Reb Shloime's children, including Adele and the Rebbetzin but not the Rebbe, and I saw all of the Zuckermans, including Chaike. Everyone was pushed toward the trucks and then thrown into them. When our turn came I was lifted up like a leaf and thrown against Fanny who fell over onto one of the Feinschmidt girls. She shrieked and cried. Chaike wailed and she wouldn't stop, so a guard hit her across the head with his rifle butt. There was a horrible squishing sound and she toppled over, her skull smashed in. Fanny clung to me. I held on to her tightly and whispered into her ear.

"Fanny. God will take care of us. Either He will spare us or He will take us; either way we're in His care. Don't be afraid."

She looked up into my eyes, and hers filled with

tears. I had always been the weak one, but she was my baby sister. I had to be strong for her, I had to be. I don't know where I found the courage. Maybe it came from God.

She nodded. "I won't be afraid," she said. Then she looked at me and said fiercely, "I'll die bravely, Marisa. They can't stop me from doing that!"

How I admired her. She would, too. I knew that. I also knew that even though I tried to look brave, I would die afraid. I tried not to cry at that thought, but tears fell down my cheeks anyway.

Finally the trucks stopped and we were pushed out. We were at the old castle. In front of the castle before the parapets was a deep ravine—what had been a moat. There were lines of German soldiers with machine guns. There was a long line of Jews. I watched as the Jews were pushed in front of the ravine, five at a time, and then the soldiers opened up on them and they dropped into the ravine. Little children, women, old men . . . Mothers begged for their children's lives, babies screamed in terror, the old men chanted the Shema. Fanny and I were near the end of the line. I wished we were near the front. Then our suffering would be over.

Fanny said, "It's the Zuckermans." I watched Chaike's mother stand by the ravine, beside her three sons and Chaike. The machine guns exploded. They cried out and then they were gone. I felt woozy and I dropped to the ground, head in between my knees. Fanny yanked me up.

"What does it matter," I snapped at her, "if they shoot us here, or there?"

"It's five more minutes alive," she said.

Five more minutes of torture, I thought, but I didn't argue with her. I could feel she was trembling. Adele and her family were shot and then others and in a couple minutes it would be our turn. It was so dark, as if the sun couldn't watch and the entire world had gone black. And then, suddenly, lightning flashed and a huge bang of thunder hit overhead. Rain started to fall. Within minutes it was pouring and fork lightning was shooting from the clouds; thunder crashed all around us.

Fanny pointed to the ravine. The soldiers were leaving! They didn't want to be out in a thunderstorm, I suppose, they might get wet—or worse yet, get struck by lightning. All of the soldiers got in their trucks and drove off. We looked around, bewildered. The widow Feinschmidt, with her four young children, marched up to us. She was carrying two babies; the other two could hardly walk, they were too little.

"Pick them up," she ordered Fanny and me. "We have a long walk back."

It took us a couple of hours to walk home through the downpour. By the time we got there the rain had stopped. We were afraid to go into the house. Would we find anyone there? Fanny went in ahead of me, then called back, "They're here. All here."

"You missed the 'action,'" Mama said. "Thank

God you weren't here. We all hid next door. I think it's over now."

"We didn't miss it, Mama," Fanny said. And then she told Mama what had happened.

Mama pulled us both to her and held us tight. I couldn't understand that the Zuckermans and the Rebbetzin and her children were now dead. I clung to Mama and breathed in the smell of the lemon-scented soap she used and I trembled so violently my teeth chattered. But I didn't cry. I was horrified into a state beyond fear. I kept hearing the crack of the guns, the screams, but instead of the Zuckermans I saw Papa and Uncle Avraham, standing by a pit, Papa praying, then the guns firing. . . . *How could I continue to live,* I wondered, *with such images etched forever in my mind?* I was sorry then that the Germans had spared me. It would have been easier to be dead, too.

"Shah," Mama said, "shah."

Was I crying after all?

FOUR

SHMUEL SURVIVED the "action," and so did his family. My mother's parents had lived in a village not far from Zloczow and they had been forced into a ghetto, but at least they were still alive. Father's father, my zaida, had died years earlier. Baba had gone to live with Mama's sister Zosia. They were both killed in the latest "action," as were my two little cousins. Mama's brother Mendel and his family were all right, but every day someone else we knew was taken, or died. We were in a constant state of grief, every night reciting the Kaddish, the prayer for the dead.

Fall turned into an early winter which came on fast and bitter. The snow lay thick on the ground; the walls were covered in frost. We had no fuel for the stove unless Yehuda and Shmuel managed to forage for bits of wood in apartments left empty by those already murdered. Sometimes I went out into the country to barter. We somehow managed to get enough food to stay alive but others were starving. Mama turned no one away—if any relative turned up at our door we fed them. I always thought we were so poor, and, of course we had turned in all our valuables, but Mama had her own money, apparently, and had hidden some valuables in the basement. She showed me where in case we needed it one day to barter for our freedom.

I didn't know how to feel about Shmuel. He was at our house often. He and Yehuda made a good team—Yehuda was small enough to crawl into spaces that Shmuel couldn't fit into and Shmuel had a knack for finding useful materials.

Actually, I was angry at Shmuel. I hadn't really spoken to him since Papa had been taken away. *If not for him,* I thought, *I never would have fought with Papa, and Papa would be with us now.* Instead, well, we hadn't heard a word from Papa. No one who was arrested that day had been heard from. The longer the silence went on, the more we all thought that those men had been murdered. Especially after the day that Fanny and I were almost shot. If they could shoot women and children they could certainly shoot grown men.

I was thinking about all of this, one cold after-noon, huddled under my quilt on the living room couch when Shmuel walked in.

"Please, Marisa, can we talk?" Shmuel asked.

I pulled the quilt over my head.

"Marisa. Please."

I pushed the covers down and sat up.

"Marisa." Sarah came in and cuddled under the quilt with me. Then Fanny did the same. Yehuda poked his head in.

"Marisa, Shmuel found us enough wood to burn for a week," Yehuda said.

"Did you?" I said, so excited that for a moment I forget to be mad at him.

He nodded.

"Marisa." Then he looked at everyone. "How can I talk to Marisa with such an audience?"

"We won't listen," Fanny said, grinning. "Go ahead."

"You won't listen?"

"No," Fanny said.

"Marisa," said Shmuel, "I wonder where Fanny got such a temper? Everyone else is so good-natured in this family."

"I do *not* have a temper," Fanny exclaimed, eyes flashing.

"Fanny," said Shmuel, "you said you weren't going to listen!"

"Oh, all right," she laughed, and she pulled Sarah and Yehuda away. "Come. We'll all cuddle up in my bed. It's nicer there, without insulting cousins hanging around."

When they were gone I spoke. "Shmuel, this is exactly what Papa didn't want—it's wrong for us to be alone together."

Shmuel sat down opposite me. "Marisa," he said, "you can be very hard."

"What do you mean?"

"I mean that you are too hard on yourself. You blame yourself for your father and you blame me. But you don't blame those who are really at fault." He paused. "I've waited and waited for you to see it isn't our fault but it seems like you never will.

Marisa, it is the *Germans*. They took your father away. And they took my father, too. Don't you think I hurt as much as you do?"

Why didn't Shmuel understand? My last words to Papa were said in anger, in defiance. I would never get the chance to tell him I was sorry. I would never have the chance to make it right.

I didn't tell Shmuel that; the words wouldn't come out. Maybe Shmuel was right but I had a block of ice around my heart, just like the snow and ice all around us. I couldn't feel anything for him anymore but anger and guilt.

"Marisa," he said, "we've cared for each other since we were little. I always thought we'd be together for our whole lives. Now the Germans have taken away our dreams, our futures." He got up and paced. "I don't want to die with you angry at me. I couldn't stand that."

Mama came into the room just then. "Marisa, I need you to help me. Shmuel, go home and get your family. With the beets I have and the wood now, I can make a nice soup. I even have two onions saved from last week."

Before I could answer Shmuel gave me one last look, a really pitiful one, and hurried out.

"He's such a good boy," Mama said. "You could do worse."

"But Papa said he didn't want me to think of him that way," I exclaimed, shocked.

Mama came over to me. She patted my hand.

"Papa felt bad about not being able to do something about the Germans. Not being able to protect you. *This* he could do something about. Let's just say he blew it out of proportion."

"You mean he really wasn't angry about Shmuel and me?"

"I didn't say that. He wouldn't have liked it no matter what. He wanted an observant boy for you. But you're young. In peaceful times his approach would have been different. Then . . . well, he was angry. Why not go and yell at his brother? And pretend it's about you when it's about all of us, and fear, and . . ." Mama's expression was so sad. "I remember what he said about not being able to protect you." Her voice cracked. "He's right, Marisa. That's the hardest thing of all for a parent." Her eyes filled with tears. She swiped her cheek with her sleeve.

"Now come and help me with dinner. We have food. That, we can be thankful for."

I went in and helped Mama. I appreciated what she'd said. I knew she didn't want me to blame myself. But no matter what they all said the facts wouldn't change. My last words to Papa had been in anger. And all over Shmuel. Those were the facts.

FIVE

WHEN SPRING THAW WAS almost over, we received word that we were to move into the ghetto in a week's time. We knew that the only reason to put us in a ghetto was so they could gather us into one spot, which made killing us easier. Then we heard that there was to be another "action" just before the move—there was always someone in the Judenrat who found out when the "actions" would take place. Fanny and I were scheduled to work on a farm to help with the seeding. We hoped that we could find somewhere to hide out there until it was all over. Mother and the little ones planned to hide next door.

Shmuel had been working in a factory for the Germans, fourteen hours a day, almost no food, and always the chance that he could be shot if a German was having a bad day. I thought a lot about the conversation we'd had. It was the last time we'd spoken privately because after that he'd been forced to spend every minute at the factory. I understood what he and Mama were trying to tell me. But I still wished I could see Papa one last time.

Every new "action" became harder than the last

one. That day I looked at little Moishe and little Sarah and at Yehuda and wondered if I'd ever see them again. And I couldn't stand the thought of them suffering when and if they died. I prayed that if it had to happen it would be quick for them. I gave them each a huge hug and a kiss. I kissed Mama lots of times and hugged her. Fanny did the same. Then we hurried out of the house while it was still dark, anxious to get to the farm by sunrise, anxious to be away when the "action" started. I hoped that Shmuel had heard about it. Often the workers from the factory were arrested in "actions"—they were so easy to find after all.

My friend Sophie came with us. We were all that was left of the original six girls: Fanny, Sophie, and me. Every day we reported to a work center and were sent somewhere. Sometimes we worked from six in the morning until eight or nine at night. I often would think of Pharaoh and Egypt, of the Jews' four hundred years of slavery. As Passover approached, the story became more and more relevant. But Pharaoh began to seem like a rather nice dictator to me—at least he hadn't set out to destroy every Jew on the face of the earth.

We spent the day turning the soil of a huge vegetable garden. We were treated quite nicely by the Polish lady, Mrs. Florczak, who knew Sophie's father. He was a butcher before the Germans stopped him from working. She fed us lunch and dinner. Just as we were about to return home I saw Shmuel running up the road. He looked awful, so thin, I could hardly recognize him as the same boy; seeing him like that broke my heart. But then I had to wonder how he had found us. What had happened? Before I could stop myself I found myself running toward him and when I reached him I threw myself into his arms. He held on to me tightly, and I could feel his face, wet with tears. I knew I had to say something to him before he spoke.

"Shmuel, it's not your fault about Papa. I know it isn't. I'm sorry. I'm sorry." And I kissed his cheeks and held his face between my hands. "What's happened?"

"They took all of the men in the factory. I hid in a box when I heard them coming. When I got home, no one was there. My family is gone. All of them. I've been going from farm to farm looking for you. I had to find you."

Fanny and Sophie ran over to us in time to overhear what he said.

"We have to go home," Fanny exclaimed. "Mama, the children!"

I caught her arm. "What if they've been taken already?" I asked. "Would Mama want us captured, too?" Releasing her, I turned and hurried over to Mrs. Florczak. "Please," I said, "may we stay here tonight? It's not safe for us back in town."

She shook her head, worried. "And if you're caught?" Sophie started to cry. I was crying, too. Fanny just looked angry. "All right, all right, there's some hay piled up near the barn," she relented. "Go there and sleep. If they find you, I know *nothing* about it, nothing."

"Thank you, thank you," I said. We found some large piles of hay and settled down in the middle of them. I wasn't sure if it was the shock, the exhaustion, or both, but Shmuel lay his head in my lap and then fell asleep immediately. I stroked his hair. Seeing him lying there so vulnerable, so thin, but still so beautiful, inspired a rush of emotion in me.

I loved him. I knew that so clearly. But there was no point to being in love, was there? We couldn't make plans, we couldn't dream of children, of a life together. There was no point in any sort of vision of the future, I realized. For instance, I had never told Papa, but I had always, more than anything, wanted to be a scholar. I had wanted to study. I'd wanted to be a teacher like him. Papa would never have approved of a woman having ideas like that, so I never told him.

"I hate God," Fanny said suddenly, vehemently, shaking me out of my reverie.

"Fanny!" I remonstrated. Shmuel stirred. "Shshsh. Don't wake Shmuel."

"I hate Him," she whispered again fiercely. "No, I don't hate Him. You can't hate what doesn't exist."

"Fanny! I can't believe I'm hearing this."

"No God would permit such evil."

"You know what the Baal Shem Tov says, Fanny," I reminded her. "'In the struggle with evil, only faith matters.'"

"Well, then," Fanny said defiantly, "what happens when you have no faith?"

"Fanny's right." Sophie sighed. "If there is a God, He's turned his back on us. I'd prefer to think there wasn't one. Otherwise He's far too cruel."

"'The blessing of the Holy One is peace.'" I quoted from the Talmud.

Fanny snorted.

"It's not God's fault that people can be so awful," I objected.

"Of course it is," Fanny countered. "He made the world. He made the rules. He could've made different ones."

I felt my throat tighten and my breath came quickly. What if Fanny and Sophie were right? It had never occurred to me to question God. *What if He is cruel?* I thought *Or could it be He hates us?*

Or is He punishing us? Or . . . or . . . He doesn't even exist?

I needed Papa. Papa could have told me. He'd have recited a wise story. He would have told me what the great thinkers had to say about evil. After all, there'd always been cruelty in the world.

But why, Papa, why?

I woke up with a start. Shmuel was sobbing beside me. It was day. Sophie and Fanny were asleep in the hay. I touched Shmuel's face. He looked up and saw I was awake. He pulled me to him and cried and then he was kissing my hair and my cheeks and his lips were on mine. He tasted of saltwater and tears; his lips were soft and sweet.

I felt a kick on my leg and we sprang apart. Fanny

was wide awake, shaking her head at us. I smiled sheepishly. Shmuel wiped his tears away.

"We should go see if your family is all right," he said, his voice shaky. We woke Sophie and the four of us walked back into town. When we reached our street it seemed deserted. Sophie ran toward her house. We ran to ours. I burst through the front door.

"Mama! Yehuda! Sarah!"

Fanny was right behind me. She raced from room to room and finally came back, shaking her head.

We hurried out into the street. Sophie ran out of her house. "My family is safe. But we go to the ghetto today. Yours?"

"No one is there," I called. I was sure they were still hiding next door, though; that had to be the explanation of the empty house. We knocked on Mr. Kraszewski's door. There was a long silence. We knocked again. The door opened a crack. Mr. Kraszewski saw us and motioned us in.

"Are they safe?" I asked, looking at him hopefully.

He motioned us to follow him to the kitchen where he had us sit down. He put bread in front of us. Shmuel grabbed some and ate hungrily. I stared at Mr. Kraszewski. Inside I repeated over and over: *There is a God. There is a God. And He has spared them. He has spared them.* "They were safe with me," Mr. Kraszewski said. "The Germans came. They took everyone they could find but they were safe here, up in the attic. Then last night they went home. And the Germans came again."

"No!" Fanny leaped up.

He shook his head. "It was terrible. Moishe and Sarah cried so loud. But Yehuda, he was a little man. He helped your mother with the children, he was a brave little one. Now all Jews not taken in the "action" have to go to the ghetto by tomorrow or they'll be shot as they stand. They won't kill everyone in the ghetto right away," he continued, his voice matter-of-fact. "They still need workers. But not for too long. After all, they have us Poles to work for them, don't they?"

He paused then, and looked at me. I was frozen like a Polish winter. I was cold right through into my bones.

"You know, Miriam," Mr. Kraszewski suggested, "you could be one of us."

I didn't respond but Shmuel did. "What do you mean?"

"Well, look at her. She looks like a Pole. And you know they are forcing Polish girls to go to Germany to work. She could do that."

"How?" Shmuel asked.

"I have a friend in Lvov," he explained. "Miriam could go there. They'll help her. She could just walk up and down the streets for a few hours, and the Germans would probably grab her. Otherwise, maybe some Polish girl can give Miriam her papers. She gets to stay home while Miriam goes. My cousin made such an arrangement with a Jewish girl only last month."

I finally found my voice. It was surprisingly

steady. And I felt nothing; no fear, no horror, nothing. "Thank you Mr. Kraszewski," I said. "You've been a good friend to our family. But we are going to stay here and wait. Maybe they've escaped. If they have they'll come back here. I'm not leaving. Not yet."

He looked at Fanny. "That might be all right for you, Miriam. Even for this boy, if you could do something about his hair. But your sister looks like a Jew. And all Jews have to be in the ghetto. If they see her, they'll shoot her."

"He's right," Fanny said. "I'm going to the ghetto with Sophie and her family if they'll have me. You have a better chance without me."

"No!" I exclaimed.

"Unless you tie me down," Fanny said, her eyes filling with tears at the thought of leaving me, "I will go. I won't put you in danger. You must do what Mr. Kraszewski suggests. Someone from our family has to survive." She glared at Shmuel. "Make sure she does. And you, too."

She took my hand. "We'll spend the day together. And tonight. But tomorrow, I'll go with Sophie."

"Here, children," Mr. Kraszewski offered, "take the bread with you." He gave us a few potatoes, too, and some carrots.

And we returned to our empty house, which was filled only with the ghosts of our family.

SIX

I TOOK OFF MY ARMBAND, went to Mama's room, and reached under her mattress where she always kept a little emergency money. To my great relief I discovered it was still there. Most of the valuables were in the basement but Mama didn't like to hide everything in one place. "If the Germans find one cache perhaps they'll miss another," she used to say.

I told Fanny and Shmuel to stay put. I braided my hair neatly, washed my face and hands, and dressed in clean clothes. Then I walked quickly down our street and turned and walked two streets over to the beauty salon. I explained to a young woman behind the cash register that I was to be married next week but that my sister looked far too dowdy. I lowered my voice and motioned her closer. "And she looks like one of those Jews, with her dark hair. We're afraid the Germans will grab her and shoot her." I made a face. "It would be just like her to ruin my wedding, the little brat."

The young woman was very sympathetic. "Nothing worse then looking like one of those filthy Jews," she said. "Here, I'll fix you up." She sold me a package of hair dye which she swore would turn even black hair blond.

I walked home as quickly as I could, terrified to be out on the street. When I got back I heard excited voices coming from the kitchen. I hurried in. And there was Yehuda.

"Yehuda!" I raced over to him and grabbed him in a huge hug. "Are you all right? Where are the others?"

His short black hair stood straight up on his head. His face was white, all the blood drained out of it, his clothes were ripped and dirty. He was covered in scratches, on his face, his hands, and his hair was encrusted with dirt.

I made him sit on the chair. I gave him some of the bread and some water.

"Yehuda," I said gently, "tell us what has happened."

Yehuda took a deep breath. When he let it out it was ragged and caught in his throat. When he spoke his voice was small, like a little child's.

"They forced us onto the streets, made us walk to the train station. Then they pushed us onto cattle cars and sealed them up. We were cramped in so tight you could hardly move but there was a window, a little window, just over where we'd been shoved. Mama made Sarah hold Moishe and then she kissed me. She said, 'God watch over you.' She waited until the train had been moving for a few minutes, until we were out of town. Then she lifted me up, you know how strong Mama is, and she pushed me out the window, headfirst. The guards saw me fall and they shot at me, but they missed. I rolled and rolled, then I scrambled up and I ran as fast as I could. Back here."

We all stared at Yehuda, speechless. It seemed like a miracle.

"Why did Mama do it?" Yehuda said, his voice gaining strength. "We're all going to die, anyway. I wanted to stay with them. I wanted to die with them."

"But now I won't be alone," Fanny said. "We'll be together."

"I'm not going to the ghetto!" Yehuda declared fiercely.

"We have no choice," Fanny replied. "Look at us. At least Marisa and Shmuel have a chance to pass as Poles."

"I'm going to the forest," Yehuda declared. "I'm going to fight with the partisans."

"You're too young," said Shmuel. "They won't want you. And you're a Jew. My friend Henryk knows all about these things. The Polish partisans hate the Jews."

"Then I'll find Jewish partisans. There *must* be some. I'd rather die in the forest, if I have to die. They shoot you there. I don't want to have to lie in a grave and be buried alive." The strength left his voice and he began to cry.

My heart hurt. If only I could comfort him the way I used to when he suffered from nightmares. But there was no comfort for this.

"I'm going with him," Fanny declared.

"Fanny," I protested, "it's different for a girl. What do you think will happen to you when the Polish partisans find you?"

"And what'll happen to me here?" she said. "The same. I'll cut my hair," she said, "and wear Yehuda's clothes. We'll be like brothers."

Because of the hunger, at thirteen Fanny was tall but not developed as a girl. I looked at Shmuel. He was the oldest. He nodded his head.

"Let them do it," he said. "We don't know if any of us will survive or who has a better chance. It's probably all luck, good or bad. So why not?"

"Let's work on you now," I said.

Fanny and I diligently applied the dye, and eventually, Shmuel's hair dried into a soft blond color. With his huge blue eyes and his height, he looked just like a Pole.

Yehuda shook his head. "You should come with us," he said to Shmuel. "You'll *never* pass as a Pole and you know why. All they have to do is pull down your pants," Yehuda reminded him. "And don't you think you'll be checked before you go into Germany? It'll never work."

I stared at Yehuda. Barely eleven now and yet he spoke like an old wise man. "Wait a minute," I protested. "I never said I'd go to Germany. I think we should all stick together. Maybe we can find someone to hide us. A farmer like Mrs. Florczak."

Just then we heard a knock at the door. It wasn't a loud banging, so it *probably* wasn't the Germans, yet we all froze.

"It's Mr. Kraszewski," a voice called. "Let me in."

"Ah, Miriam," he said when I opened the door. "I may have something to help you. Some friends I know, their daughter has been called to work, forced labor, in Germany. If you have a little something, money, jewels, you might be able to buy her papers. She will cease to exist—you will go to Poland in her place. And her name is Maria. So God must have meant for you to do it."

"I don't know," I said, hesitantly. "I don't want to leave my family."

"Miriam," he said, "your people are doomed. All Jews are doomed. But with your looks you might just make it."

"All right, thank you, Mr. Kraszewski. Thank you."

He reached out and patted my shoulder. "I'm sorry it's come to this," he said. "I'm a military man. I understand war. But this kind of murder, I can't understand. And to see military men carrying it out and disgracing themselves . . ." He shook his head and walked away, muttering.

I returned to the kitchen and told the others what he'd said. I realized that I now had to make the hardest decision of my life. I wanted to stay with Fanny and Yehuda and Shmuel. I didn't want to be on my own. The thought terrified me. But I knew Yehuda was right. Shmuel couldn't come with me. And I couldn't get rid of one thought: *Will no one from our family survive? God willing, Fanny and Yehuda might succeed. But if they don't? And* then I wondered if I weren't better suited to deception than to life as a partisan. I was smart, after all, and I could learn German. I could work hard. I might be able to fool everyone. At least I could try.

"Marisa?" Yehuda broke into my thoughts. I had almost forgotten anyone else was in the room. I looked at them all. How could I desert them? I was the older sister.

Shmuel took me by the hand and pulled me into the other room.

"Marisa," he said, his voice stern, "you will *not* be deserting them."

"How did you know that's what I was thinking?"

"It's obvious. It's what I would be thinking. But they are probably safer without you. They are both quick and brave. They will live on their instincts. You'll only slow them down."

I managed a small smile. "Are you saying I'm slow and cowardly?"

He put his arms around me. "You are careful, and thoughtful, and *very* brave."

"You know I'm not brave," I cried, burying my head in his shoulder. "How can I go on?"

"You *must,*" he said. "We can't let them win. "*Judenfrei.* Jew-free," he repeated bitterly. "Henryk told me that there are competitions now between towns to see which will be free of Jews first. Many of the towns aren't waiting for the Germans to do it. They are killing all the Jews themselves so they can put their sign up as you enter: 'Jew-free.'"

"But I don't want to be the only one of my family

left," I protested. "I want to die with my family if they are to die."

"I'm the only one of my family left," Shmuel said quietly. "If I can stand it, so can you. We have each other. Maybe God means for us to survive together."

"I'll decide by morning," I said. "I want to think some more."

We returned to the others. I cooked up the potatoes and onions, and we ate it with the bread that was left. Then Fanny and I snuggled together in our bed, Shmuel and Yehuda sleeping in Mama's room.

Just before Fanny fell asleep she said, "You should go to Germany, Marisa. It's almost funny. Going *there* to survive."

"Shshsh," I whispered. "Get some sleep. Our last night in our own beds."

I was exhausted. I could feel myself dropping off. *Maybe,* I thought, *I should tell them I'm going, but throw myself under a train instead. I'm not brave. How can I find the courage to go on? How?*

SEVEN

PAPA CALLED ME INTO HIS STUDY.

"Sit down, Marisa," he said.

"Papa!" I cried. "You're alive! I'm so happy."

"I'm not alive in that way, Marisa," he answered gently. "But I'm still alive. And I am here to remind you of something. All the strength you need is within you, words you have studied from the Torah." Then he winked. "And the Talmud. You think I didn't know? You remember what the Baal Shem Tov said? 'When God wants to punish a man, He deprives him of faith.' But God will not punish you so. 'The righteous shall live by his faith.' I will be with you, Marisa. And God is always with you.

"Bahya said, 'The nearer the relation to the murdered person, the more heinous the crime . . . and man is closest to himself.' You must never think of taking your own life, Marisa. Promise."

"But Papa, I want to be with you."

"I am never away from you."

"It's my fault. . . ."

"Marisa! Marisa! Wake up!" It was Fanny. I woke with a start. I'd been dreaming. Dreaming. But it had felt so real. And I was finally going to apologize.

"Fanny," I snapped, "how could you! Leave me alone! I want to go back to sleep!"

"Marisa, I had a dream. Mama spoke to me. She said we must leave, now. Now. The morning will be too late!"

Both Papa and Mama speaking to us in our dreams. I took great heart from this. Perhaps we would survive, after all. Perhaps we weren't meant to die. Not just yet, anyway.

There was no time left to organize papers. My decision had been made for me. I ran down to the basement. There was an old broken chest of drawers which stood propped up in a corner. Mama had had a false bottom made in it; she'd shown me everything. In there she'd put all her jewelry and some cash. I grabbed it all and put it in my sweater pocket. I hurried upstairs.

"Take your jackets," I instructed everyone. "It'll be cold at night." I looked at Fanny. She had dressed herself in Yehuda's clothes and pulled her hair back under a cap. She really did look like his older brother.

"Let's go."

We snuck out of the house as quietly as we could and headed toward Mrs. Florczak's farm. The town was quiet, although in the distance we could hear the roar of planes. We managed to get into the country without incident but when we got to the farm, Mrs. Florczak refused to let us stay.

"They came here and warned us," she said in a whisper. "The ghetto is being made today and we are to hide no one. You can't stay here. You'll put my family in danger."

"It's almost light," I pleaded. "If we travel now we'll be caught. Please, let us stay one night. In the barn, not in the house."

For one agonizing moment she didn't reply. Finally she sighed. "All right. *One* night."

We settled ourselves in the hay at the top of the barn. We were all tired and frightened and as of that moment, we were homeless. And we were orphans. Yet we knew it could be worse. I tried to get the image out of my mind of Moishe—little Moishe with his mischievous smile, always climbing things he wasn't supposed to climb and tumbling off miraculously unscathed—this image of him lying in a ditch, clutching Mama as dirt fell on them, more and more until he couldn't breathe; him gasping for air but dirt pouring into his throat instead; he was choking, I was choking, I tried to scream, but my throat was clogged. . . .

"Marisa! Wake up. You're dreaming. You're crying out! Shshsh." Shmuel was shaking me. I was bathed in sweat, soaked, and I couldn't catch my breath.

"Slowly," he said, "slowly. Take a breath. Now another. There. There. What was it?"

"Moishe," I whispered, "I saw him buried alive."

"It was just a dream," Shmuel said.

"No," I said, "it's how they died. I know it is. A bullet was too good for them."

"Shsh," he whispered. "Go back to sleep." I glanced over at Yehuda and Fanny. They were still fast asleep. "I can't sleep. I can't," I whispered back. "I might dream again."

"Come here," Shmuel said, and he pulled me to him so that my head rested on his shoulder, his arm circling my back.

"Close your eyes. Remember this passage from Psalms? I helped you study it."

How could I forget? I was determined to memorize as much as I could, the way the boys did when they studied and Shmuel hadn't laughed at me. He had taken me seriously. Even though he could barely read the Hebrew text he had struggled through it with me. And we went over it so many times that soon we both knew it by heart. He began to recite to me, in the Hebrew:

> *Happy is the man who has not followed the*
> *counsel of the wicked,*
> *or taken the path of sinners,*
> *or joined the company of the insolent;*
> *rather, the teaching of the Lord is his delight,*
> *and he studies that teaching day and night.*
> *He is like a tree planted beside streams*
> *of water,*
> *which yields its fruit in season.*
> *Whose foliage never fades,*
> *and whatever it produces thrives.*

"You'll be like that Marisa," he said gently. "When this is over you'll be a great scholar. You will honor your father's name."

"Recite some more," I said. "Do you remember?"

"How could I not?" he smiled, probably thinking

about that day, too, a quiet day, sitting on our front steps watching Moishe and Sarah play as the grown-ups talked at the kitchen table.

He continued:

> *Not so the wicked,*
> *Rather, they are like chaff that wind*
>   *blows away*
> *therefore the wicked will not survive*
>   *judgment,*
> *nor will sinners, in the assembly of*
>   *the righteous.*
> *For the Lord cherishes the way of*
>   *the righteous,*
> *but the way of the wicked is doomed.*

"But it isn't true, is it?" I interrupted him, suddenly agitated. "The wicked are thriving, and *we* are doomed."

"Marisa, you're a scholar and I'm not. But don't you think this means in the world to come? The souls of the wicked will not survive judgment."

"But Jews don't believe in hell," I objected. "So what does this really mean?"

"Maybe," said Fanny, her voice sleepy, "it means that even here on earth their souls are dammed. How black their souls must be. I'd rather be dead than be them."

"She's right," Shmuel agreed. "Because later it says:

> *For there is not sincerity on their lips;*
> *Their heart is filled with malice;*
> *Their throat is an open grave;*

Their tongue slippery.

Shmuel faltered. "How does the rest go?"
I took up the recitation:

Condemn them, O God;

Yehuda and Fanny joined in:

Let them fall by their own devices;
Cast them out for their many crimes,
For they defy you.
But let all that take refuge in you rejoice. . . .

"Shah," said Fanny.

Just then someone opened the barn door. It was one of Mrs. Florczak's daughters come to milk the cows. The children couldn't know we were there, they could easily give us away.

It seemed to take her forever to do the milking. When she was finally gone we relaxed, a little. But in the quiet of the morning we could hear shots in the distance.

I ran down to the barn and found an old bucket and brought it back up. Each of us took turns using it in the corner. I was so horribly embarrassed to do such a thing even *near* Shmuel, I could feel my face turning bright red. It was so humiliating. But what choice did we have? Those not using the bucket tried to talk to keep the sound out of our ears and make the person using it less uncomfortable.

It was a long day. We had no food, no water. Finally, as night descended Mrs. Florczak came into the barn.

"Time to leave," she called.

We scrambled down the ladder. She had some bread and cheese with her and a flask of water. She was obviously frightened.

"Last week Mr. Krysanska, our neighbor, was discovered hiding a Jew," she said. "The Germans took both him and the Jew to the town square. They shot the Jew. Then they cut off Mr. Krysanska's tongue. They pulled out his fingernails one by one. Then his toenails. They pulled his teeth out, gouged out his eyes; they peeled his skin off his body. They made us all watch. Everyone from the surrounding farmland and the village. Anyone who didn't watch would be shot. When we cried they laughed and threatened us with the same. And then they told us that anyone found hiding a Jew would be shot, along with their family and their ten closest neighbors. So even if someone was hiding a Jew, a neighbor would force them to turn him in. You see what we're all up against."

She sighed. "Every Jew is in the ghetto now, or dead." She looked at me and Shmuel. "You two, you could pretend to be Polish. Who would know?"

"We can't leave my brother and sister," I said. "Thank you for hiding us and for the food." We left and walked down the road going north.

"Maybe we *should* go to the ghetto," I said. "No one will hide us now."

"No," said Yehuda. "Once we're there they can kill us easily."

"Maybe we're better off somewhere where we can at least be fed," I suggested.

"No!" Yehuda insisted.

"We'll try another farm," Shmuel said. "Best to stay as far away from the Germans as possible."

We reached the next farm in about half an hour. "You two stay here," Shmuel said to the children. "Marisa and I will ask for help."

We walked up to the farmhouse and knocked. An old woman answered.

"Grandmother," said Shmuel in perfect Polish, "my little sister and I are orphans from the shooting when the Germans came to town. Please may we sleep in your barn tonight? We can work for you, too, if you need help. My sister is a very good cook and I am very strong."

She nodded her head. "All right," she says, "you can stay. But who's that?"

"They, too, are orphans we met along the road. They could sleep in the barn. They'd be no trouble."

"Let me see them."

We motioned for Yehuda and Fanny to come into the light of the lamp she was holding.

"Jews!" she hissed. "They're Jews. And so are you, no doubt."

"Please," I pleaded, "we won't hurt anything. We just need a place to stay."

"Never! I have a family. Now get away! Get away!"

We turned and moved off but I was beginning to feel trapped like an animal being hunted. All the farmers would react the same way, and finally the Germans would catch us.

If we didn't find some cover soon we would certainly be discovered. There was a hay shed on the edge of the property we were on.

"Let's hide in there for the day," I suggested. "We'll think what to do tonight."

We took off the roof of the shed and jumped down into it. We made little beds for ourselves in the hay, and even though I was afraid to sleep, in case I dreamed, I fell asleep before I could even speak to the others.

EIGHT

"SHAH, SHE'S WAKING UP."

When I opened my eyes Fanny and Yehuda were staring at me. Fanny grinned as if she had been caught doing something wrong. Yehuda's face was a mask of feigned indifference.

"What are you two up to?" I asked, suspicious.

"Nothing," said Fanny, "we're hungry that's all. Where will we go tonight?"

I glanced at Shmuel. He was wide awake.

"I think we should stay here," he said. "No one has found us. Fanny and Yehuda should stay, while you and I go and beg some food."

"Not from this farmer," I said.

"No, no, from another. We'll use the same story as last time."

"Don't move from here," I ordered the children as Shmuel and I set off. We walked to a farmer's house a few miles off, an enormous one with a huge barn. He answered the door himself. He looked at us with displeasure but people around there rarely said no to the needy (so long as they weren't Jews). He let us come in and gave us each a cup of sour milk.

"We should be going," I said as we stood in the

kitchen. "We can take the milk with us if you have an old bottle."

"No, no, eat it here," he insisted.

I felt horrible spooning up what should go to Fanny and Yehuda but not eating wouldn't help them. Shmuel and I ate slowly, savoring every bite.

"May we take some bread?" I asked boldly as we finished.

He nodded and sliced some pieces for us. "Eat," he said.

"No, we'll eat as we go. We have relatives to find. May we take some water from the well?"

He gave us a small tin cup for the water and we helped ourselves with the pump. We couldn't walk back to the haystack too quickly or we'd spill the water, and by the time we got there hours had passed. Fanny and Yehuda were sitting against the shed, gazing at the stars. They ate the bread and drank the water.

"I'm still hungry," Fanny complained. "We can't live on that."

"I have Mama's jewels," I said, "but I think they'd make the farmers *very* suspicious of us, so for the moment we'll have to continue this way." I glanced at Shmuel. "Tomorrow is the first night of Passover. We'll collect as much food as we can after dark and then we'll have our own little seder. How's that?"

The idea seemed to cheer up Yehuda and Fanny. We stayed awake the rest of the night, Shmuel and I telling stories to pass the time.

We spent the day trying to sleep and then

Shmuel and I ventured out. We walked to still a different farmhouse, this one set back from the road—a small house and a neat barn. The lights were on. Shmuel knocked on the door. The door opened and an SS officer in full Nazi dress stared at both of us.

"Yes?"

For a moment, Shmuel and I were so stunned neither of us spoke, then the full force of our bad luck hit me. An SS officer would surely discover us as Jews. He'd shoot us on the spot . . . and Fanny and Yehuda would be left alone. I broke out into a sweat, I felt horribly dizzy, and then everything went black.

"Maria. Maria."

Who was Maria?

"Wake up, Maria."

I opened my eyes to see the SS officer gazing down on me, Shmuel beside him.

"There, you'll be fine!" Shmuel declared. "I've explained that we're orphans traveling to Warsaw to be with an aunt and uncle. Here, can you get up?"

A young, very pretty woman peeked her head around the door.

"Poor thing. Carry her in, lie her on the couch here."

Shmuel glanced at the SS officer. He nodded. Shmuel lifted me up and carried me into the house. I was put on the couch. I could see into the dining room where an intimate dinner had obviously been in progress.

"My husband was killed in the first days of the

bombing," the woman commiserated with us. "I've been on my own for two and half years now." It was almost as if she were explaining the Nazi's presence to us.

"She was hungry," Shmuel explained. "That's why she fainted. We haven't eaten all day."

"Let me get you some milk," the woman offered.

She hurried to the kitchen and came back with two tall glasses of milk. We took them and drank without question. We couldn't afford to do anything that would make the Nazi suspicious.

"You must eat something, too," she declared.

Again, she rushed out, only to bustle back in with a plate of cheese and bread and salami.

I stared at the salami. I'd never put anything that wasn't kosher into my mouth. But if I didn't eat it, I could give us away. I knew that according to Jewish law you were allowed to eat unkosher food if it meant saving your life.

"Thank you," I said, my voice weak. "I'm sorry to have caused such a fuss. We really don't want to trouble you."

"Not at all," she said. "You eat up. Then why don't you go sleep in the back room for tonight? You can carry on to Warsaw tomorrow."

This obviously didn't please the SS officer, but I could tell that he was there to impress the young woman. When they spoke she used perfect German. She said something to him. He shrugged and replied, something about how kind she was being to a couple of lowly, stupid Poles.

Her face flushed. His expression changed and softened.

"Go ahead," he conceded.

"I'm a good Christian," she said in Polish to us. "I came here from Germany to marry my Polish husband."

Now I understood why the Nazi was there. She really wasn't a Pole, she was German.

"No, really," I said, "we couldn't impose. We don't want to lose any time."

"But you can't walk at night!" she insisted. "I won't hear of it. Gustav, you won't hear of it, either, will you?"

"Certainly not," he said, looking at us with eyes so cold they could freeze you.

I tried to force the panic away. What would Fanny and Yehuda think? They'd worry terribly. And the longer we were there, the greater the chance that the Nazi would question us or become suspicious. I wanted to run away from him as fast as I could. I had to use every bit of control not to bolt right then. I knew, though, that running would only get us shot so I forced myself to be calm.

We ate the bread and cheese and I made myself eat the salami which actually tasted delicious, I was so hungry. She took us into the back room where there were a couple of old sofas.

"You can lie down on those," she said. "In the morning you'll have a nice big breakfast."

"Thank you, Madam," I said.

"Frau Willheim," she corrected me. "You're welcome."

She and her Nazi went back to the dining room. I heard them talk, clink glasses, laugh. I wished I could tell her what her Nazi had done to my Moishe, my Sarah, my mama, my papa. To Shmuel's family. Maybe she wouldn't have cared even if she knew. But I think she would have. I looked at Shmuel. He shrugged and motioned for me to lie down.

"There's nothing we can do," he whispered. "Yehuda and Fanny are very clever. They'll stay put, don't worry. And we'll ask for lots of food tomorrow."

We lay down and I tried to sleep. But I had slept most of the day away and I was wide awake. So I lay quietly, eyes closed. At one point the Nazi did come and check on us.

"They seem harmless enough," he said, "but I'd like to see their papers."

"Don't wake them," she pleaded. "Look at them. They're exhausted. Let's sit outside and finish our wine. It's such a beautiful night."

I could hardly catch my breath after they left. Papers. Why hadn't he asked us for papers right away? He must've truly been smitten with that woman. She *was* beautiful. She looked like she should be sitting in a fancy Berlin restaurant, not living on some farm in Poland. I suppose the Nazi couldn't believe his good luck.

He left very late and the house became quiet. I must have dozed off because the cock crowing woke me up. Our hostess hurried in to the kitchen, and I could smell that she was cooking.

"Come, come," she said. "My German friend has exempted me from the quota this week, so we can eat the eggs and bacon ourselves!"

Bacon. Well, I'd already eaten the salami, and I didn't want her to become suspicious of me. I ate it. It was very good. Salty. Shmuel ate it, too.

We told her that we had to be on our way. "Could we take a little food with us for the trip?" I asked.

"Of course!" She gave me bread, cheese, and a bottle of milk.

We thanked her and walked back toward the hay shed. She called after us.

"But that's the wrong way. To Warsaw you must go that way."

"Come on," Shmuel said, "we'll have to double back behind the farm."

It took us hours of walking to finally reach the shed. But we couldn't approach it because workers were out in the fields, plowing and seeding. There was nothing to do but continue to walk the other way, as if we were actually going somewhere.

"Make a poem for me," I said to Shmuel, in an effort to take our minds off worrying about the children. Shmuel had this uncanny ability to create things spontaneously. It was never the kind of learning Papa valued but it always amazed me. He had dreamed of being a writer someday, perhaps being published. I pushed that thought of the future away. "Just make up something about right now, right here."

Shmuel thought for a few minutes. He gazed around for inspiration and then slowly began to speak:

> *Farmers plant for a new spring,*
> *green shoots will push up through the dirt,*
> *Flowers will open like a newborn baby's mouth*
> *   waiting for milk,*
> *birds will make nests, young lovers will twist*
> *   daisy chains.*
> *Children are buried alive.*
> *Where is the flood?*
> *Where is the city turning into salt? Where are*
> *   the ten plagues, locusts, hail, water turning*
> *   to blood?*
> *Where is God?*

I looked at him.

"How do you do it?" I wondered.

"I don't know how you sit over your books for hours on end studying the smallest Talmudic problem," he said, returning the compliment. "Want to hear another one?"

"Yes."

He looked more serious, thought, and then recited:

> *Hitler is a dirty rat,*
> *I hate him more than your old cat;*
> *When the war is finally done,*
> *We'll make sure he never has any fun!*

I burst out laughing, then stopped myself with a gasp of air. *What kind of person am I?* I wondered. *How can I laugh when half of my family has just been murdered? There must be something wrong with me.*

Finally it was the supper hour and the fields began to empty out as people headed home. My legs felt like they were going to crumple underneath me. I couldn't walk another step. Shmuel had to half carry me over to the shed.

"Yehuda, Fanny," I called softly. "It's only us. We're back." There was no answer. I lifted myself up and looked down into the shed. It was empty!

NINE

"THEY'VE BEEN CAPTURED! They've been captured!"

I looked around frantically. "Where are they? Oh God, please God, don't take them, too. Please God."

"Marisa," said Shmuel, holding me hard by the shoulders, "God isn't taking them. The Germans are."

I stared at him. Why was he lecturing me? I didn't have time to debate about God. The children were missing! "Leave me alone!" I shouted at him. "We have to *do* something. Find them."

"We can't go running off and put ourselves in danger, too," he said. "We have to stay calm. And, Marisa, if you pray to God to save them and He doesn't then eventually you'll lose your faith. And that's all you have. I won't let you lose it," he said fiercely.

"Why do you care?" I asked. "You've been brought up without faith and it hasn't hurt you."

"Marisa," Shmuel said, obviously upset, "that isn't true. My father didn't believe in the rules, he wasn't observant, but you know very well that he still made me go to Hebrew school. And I've wrestled with the idea of God and if there is one or not. And,

I suppose, I don't know. How could I know? But I understand one thing very well—if God exists you can't beg Him for personal favors. That wouldn't make any sense. But you can thank Him for what you have."

"Thank Him? You're joking, right?" I said.

"I've never been more serious."

"What do we have Shmuel?"

"We have love in our hearts, not hate," Shmuel answered. "And that's enough of a reason to thank Him. Even if we lose each other, or the children, or our lives, we'll still have love in our hearts and a million Nazis can never take that away from us."

"We won't have love," I muttered. "At least I won't. I *hate* the Germans."

"You don't have to," he said.

"You don't *choose* how you feel," I objected, "you just feel."

"You *can* choose," Shmuel said. "You can and you *must*."

"Marisa!"

I whirled around. Fanny and Yehuda were running toward us through the field.

"Fanny! Yehuda!"

As soon as they reached us, I grabbed them both.

"What happened to you? Where did you go? I should spank both of you right now! No, I should let Shmuel spank you so it really hurts! Get in the shed right away."

We clambered in and settled ourselves in the hay.

"We thought you'd been captured," Yehuda explained. "And we got too hungry to stay here."

"Fanny," I reprimanded her, "you should have made Yehuda stay. You're the oldest."

"I was hungry," she said defiantly.

"Did you get any food?" Shmuel asked.

Yehuda shook his head. "No one would feed us. They knew right away we were Jews."

"That's all right, Yehuda," I said, giving him a kiss, "we have food! Lots of food! We'll have our seder now."

"Marisa," said Fanny, gazing at the food, "look how well you and Shmuel do on your own. We're just going to drag you down. And soon, we'll all be caught. You and Shmuel can pretend you're Poles. Or you can go back to town and let Mr. Kraszewski help you get papers. He said he would."

"I won't leave you," I said. "You'd starve without us. You just proved it. We can keep on this way."

"We can't hide here forever," Fanny retorted. "You know that. They'll come for this hay to feed the animals, and put fresh hay in here. And what about winter? When it's so cold?"

"I won't discuss it," I said curtly. I couldn't. How could I bear to let them go off on their own like that? What kind of an older sister would I be? "We'll have our seder now."

"But, Marisa," Fanny objected, "Yehuda and I can go to the forest. We *want* to fight."

"No! I won't hear of it," I declared. "Now eat your food."

"First the seder, then the seder meal," Yehuda said.

"But you two must be starving," I said.

"I don't care. Another hour won't make any difference," Yehuda said. "Marisa, you know the service by heart; I know you do. Will you conduct it?" he asked solemnly.

One of the first prayers was the Shehecheyanu. "'Blessed is the Lord our God, Ruler of the universe, for giving us life, for sustaining us, and for enabling us to reach this day.'"

"I want each of you to promise me something," Shmuel said after I'd recited it. "No matter what happens, you will say this prayer every day."

Surprisingly both Yehuda and Fanny agreed without question.

"Marisa, won't you promise?" Fanny said.

"I'm surprised you will," I answered.

"Do you think Mama could have talked to me in a dream and warned us," Fanny said, "if she wasn't with God now?"

I thought about my dream and Papa. "I'll try," I said. "I'll try."

Yehuda, being the youngest, recited the four questions, beginning with "Why is this night different from all other nights." And then I answered him: "We were slaves of Pharaoh in Egypt; and Eternal our God brought us out from there. . . ."

I felt comforted as I chanted the service. It was our own, and the Germans couldn't take it away from us. We recited the ten plagues God inflicted on

Pharaoh so he would let the Jews go. How I wished that God would inflict them on Germany now.

Blood. Frogs. Lice. Beasts. Plagues. Boils. Hail. Locusts. Darkness. Slaying of the firstborn.

It seemed, though, that the Jewish people were enduring all ten plagues and worse. Maybe we *were* being punished.

"I won't eat the bread," Yehuda declared when the service was over. "We can't eat bread during Passover."

"And why is that?" Shmuel asked.

"To remember. The Jewish people didn't have time for the bread to rise when they escaped from Egypt so they ate unleavened bread. We've already gone over that."

"And do you think we have to be reminded what it is to be a slave? To suffer?" Shmuel demanded.

"No," Yehuda answered meekly.

"Then eat your bread."

I wished Papa could have heard Shmuel. He reasoned like a scholar, even if he wasn't the kind of scholar Papa wanted for me.

The children ate the cheese and bread and drank the milk. We assured them that we had eaten already although morning seemed a very long time ago.

When our service was over I could barely keep my eyes open. Shmuel and I had been walking all day and with nothing to eat since breakfast we were both exhausted. We each had a few sips of the milk and then we closed our eyes. I remembered I hadn't given Yehuda or Fanny a good-night kiss but I couldn't open my eyes or lift a muscle. Within seconds I was in a deep sleep.

"Marisa!" It was Shmuel.

"What is it?"

"Marisa, wake up. I'm so sorry."

"What? What?" I opened my eyes and I saw right away why he was apologizing. The children were gone.

"I've checked outside," he said. "I can't see them anywhere."

"Why didn't we hear them go?" I cried. "How could they sneak off like that?"

"We must've been so tired from all that walking. . . ."

"They've gone to the forest. They've left us, thinking we can survive better without them."

"Yes."

"How *could* they?" I paused. "Do you think we could find them?"

"We can try."

It was still dark. There was a forest a few miles to the north and one about ten miles to the east.

"Which way?" I asked as we climbed out of the shed.

"They might actually head for the forest farther away," Shmuel said, "to fool us."

I sighed. "We'll never find them." Tears welled up in my eyes. "Will we?"

"Marisa, they're your family. I'll do what you say."

"I wish I knew how long they've been gone. Then we'd know if we had a chance of catching them."

"They probably left as soon as we fell asleep—and judging from the moon that could have been six or seven hours ago. It will be daylight soon."

I looked around at the dark, the silence. . . .

"How could they!"

"Marisa," Shmuel said, taking my hand, "it's what they wanted. And they're both smart, and quick. Fanny looks just like a boy in those clothes." He paused, then shook his head. "Stupid little children!"

He was just as upset as I was. They were the only family the two of us had left. I thought back to the whispered conversation they'd been having and realized that they'd probably been thinking about this for a while.

"We'll go back to town," I decided, "and see if Mr. Kraszewski can help us. We'll never find them now."

We really weren't that far away from town. By dawn we were there. We walked confidently, holding hands, as if we had nothing to fear. We reached Mr. Kraszewski's without incident.

He answered the door and seemed shocked to see us.

"Ghosts," he said, "I'm looking at ghosts. I thought the Germans had got you."

"We escaped just before they came," I answered.

"Come in, come in," he said. "Where are the little ones?"

"They've run off to join the partisans in the forest."

"They have pluck," he said gravely. "Courage. Would you still like those papers?" he asked hopefully. "Maria is set to leave tomorrow and hasn't been able to find anyone to take her place. All the Jews are dead or in the ghetto now, and of course they aren't allowed to leave the ghetto."

I looked at Shmuel. He nodded.

"Yes, Mr. Kraszewski," I answered. "I'll take the papers. I'll go in her place."

TEN

MR. KRASZEWSKI GOT the papers for me. I became Maria Sliwowska, eighteen years old, birthday March 21, the first day of spring.

He also had a further plan for me. He urged me to report to the center in Lvov rather than the one in our hometown. He was afraid someone in Zloczow would recognize me. Also, he hoped his friends in Lvov might be able to help me—even put me up or employ me so that I wouldn't actually have to go into Germany. I was to catch the first morning train for Lvov.

Shmuel decided to stay with his Polish friend Henryk, posing as a Pole. Henryk was considering volunteering for work in Germany; his father had been arrested; his mother, a nurse, was already in Germany, forced to work there; and his sisters were staying with a hated aunt. For the moment, though, he felt safe enough. Shmuel said that if Henryk went to Germany he would go, too.

It was time for me to leave. Shmuel and I stared at each other. Would we ever see each other again, in this life? He drew me to him and whispered in my ear, "Remember, love in your heart, not hate."

"I'll try," I whispered back.

Then he was gone. And I was alone. All alone.

"Go on, Miriam," Mr. Kraszewski said. "You must get going."

I realized that I still had the jewels from Mama.

"Mr. Kraszewski," I asked, "will you keep these for me?"

"I'll try to save them for you," he answered.

"But if you need to use them, for a bribe or anything, you go right ahead." Impulsively I threw my arms around his neck and kissed both his cheeks. "What a good friend you've been," I said.

"Without your parents hiding me," he replied, "I'd be in Siberia now, or worse. We've helped each other, that's all. Now hurry up."

When I reached the train station it was packed with people. I bought a ticket but the train had been delayed. I waited for hours, and for every minute of that time I was sure I'd be discovered. At around noon, I noticed a Pole going through the crowd. He was looking at each face closely. I realized that he was probably looking for Jews like me trying to escape. He would be paid for finding them. My heart started to pound. Casually I moved away from him. I wandered into the station, trying to look relaxed, and I went to the ladies' room. I decided to wait there in a stall. Finally I heard the train for Lvov being announced. I took a deep breath, then walked purposefully through the station and boarded immediately.

I sat down beside a girl a few years older than me. She was very beautiful and was nicely dressed.

She looked clean and well fed. The train started to move. Somehow, I had managed it so far. I stuck my hands in my pockets. And then my heart sank. I was wearing my favorite sweater: a thick, cream-colored cardigan of pure wool. But I'd forgotten that I always carried a picture of Mama in that sweater. She used to put it in there so I wouldn't be afraid. "Just touch it," she'd say, "and it'll be as if I am there with you. If a bully scares you or a nasty dog barks at you, just remember I'll be there!" I used to laugh and say, "Mama, will your picture come to life and protect me, like a golem?" And she'd put her hands in the air like a monster, and say, "Yes, I will! I will!"

But her picture wouldn't protect me anymore. In fact, it would kill me. What if I was searched? It was so obviously a picture of a Jewish woman. How could I get rid of it? Slowly, I took it out of my pocket. I crumpled it and held it in my fist. Then I got up and walked to the end of the compartment. I looked around. The train was jammed with people, and a number of German soldiers. I felt that everyone was watching me, so I couldn't just drop it. The train rocked and I fell over almost on top of an older woman. Without giving myself time to think I dropped the picture just behind her, excused myself and hurried back to my seat.

The train usually took an hour and a half to get to Lvov but we were still traveling when it got dark.

"There's a Jew on this train!"

I gasped involuntarily and clasped my hands together so they wouldn't shake.

An inspector was holding up my mother's picture for all to see, shining his flashlight on it. He began to walk up and down the aisles. "Papers. Papers."

"I saw you take that photo out of your pocket," the girl next to me said. "Don't worry. I won't give you away."

"Thank you," I whispered.

The inspector flashed the light in our faces and checked our papers. He nodded with approval at us, then moved on.

"'For what shall it profit a man, if he shall gain the whole world, and lose his own soul?' St. Mark said that," my neighbor whispered. "The Germans have lost their souls. I pity them."

I remembered Shmuel's admonition to me and I realized that there *was* something to thank God for. *Thank you God,* I said to myself, *for not making me like them.*

The girl squeezed my hand. "Take heart. Goodness lives."

Perhaps she was an angel. I closed my eyes and drifted off to sleep.

The train pulled into the Lvov station at five A.M. I didn't want to wander the streets in the dark so I sat on a bench in a corner and pretended to sleep. When day broke I ventured out into the city.

I had to ask directions often and after a very long walk I finally reached Grodaska Street. But the people Mr. Kraszewski told me about were no longer there. A neighbor shook his head as I knocked on the door for the fourth time.

"No use," he said. "They were taken away. He taught at the University, you know. Professors were the first the Germans took."

For a moment I stood there discouraged and unable to think of what to do. Then I remembered that Mr. Kraszewski's first idea had been for me to go directly to the foreign workers' center in Lvov. I decided that I had no other choice. I asked the neighbor if he knew the way to the center. He did and he even volunteered to walk me part of the way there so I wouldn't get lost. Within an hour I was standing outside what looked to be an old army barracks. There were thousands of people waiting to be transported. I was processed and put into a barracks with hundreds of other girls.

That night, as I was falling asleep, I heard someone cry out in Yiddish. I looked around but didn't see the supervisor. Quickly I got up and walked down the aisles. Again she cried out. I kicked her, hard.

"What?" she said, waking up.

"You're dreaming in Yiddish," I whispered to her in Polish. "Stay awake or you'll be caught."

I hurried back to my bunk just as the female supervisor came in, cup of tea in hand. I held my breath. Why did I do that? Any girl seeing me would surely give me away, turn me in. After all, why help a Jew unless you're a Jew, too? I tried to slow my breathing. I remembered what Papa had said in the dream. "Think of the Torah for comfort." *Should I have let her die to save myself?* I wondered. The

Talmud said, "A person is always liable for his actions, whether awake or asleep." My breath slowed down. *I did the right thing,* I thought, *made the right choice. The outcome is for God to decide.*

The room was silent. No one spoke up against me, or the other girl. I sighed and closed my eyes. And prayed that I wouldn't cry out in Yiddish in my sleep.

After a few long days in the camp, just waiting, doing nothing, we were finally loaded into trains. It was a long trip. It took two days before we crossed the border into Germany. Just over the border we were taken off the train for medical inspection. We were moved into the showers first. Then our hair was checked for lice. Thank God I didn't have any. Those who did had their hair shaved and disinfectant poured all over them. Then we were forced to stand naked, about fifty of us, while a team of doctors and nurses checked us over. They listened to our chests, our hearts, checked our skin for rashes, took our temperatures. At least three different doctors checked me. How would Shmuel survive this inspection? He couldn't and I hoped he wouldn't even try. The Germans may have wanted workers but it must have also been true what Mama had said: They wanted everything to be clean. I got a picture in my mind of all the blood that had been spilled over the last two and a half years. I wished I could have put it in a giant balloon and that I could have floated the balloon over Germany and then slashed it with a big sword so that blood would have poured over everyone and then we'd see how clean they felt.

When the medical inspection was over and we were dressed, all the girls were taken into a large room. We were forced to stand there as one by one we were interrogated. It was almost my turn when the young girl being questioned ahead of me started to cry.

"I'm not a Jew."

"Look at you!"

She had black hair, brown eyes, and a delicate face. "I can't help that I'm dark. Papa is dark, his family is like that. Look at my papers." Hands trembling, she showed them her papers.

"You could have stolen them from someone! How do we know they're real?" He took them. "Quickly, what is your mother's name?"

"Zosia."

"Your father's?"

"Mlot."

"Where were you born?"

"Kielce."

They kept peppering her with questions, and even though she had tears running down her face she answered them all correctly.

The man thrust the papers back at her. "All right. I suppose you just have the bad luck to look like one of them."

I felt like saying, "Look at Hitler. Dark hair, dark mustache, he doesn't look like his Aryan ideal." But of course I said nothing.

When it was my turn I smiled prettily and handed over my papers.

He looked at me approvingly, then at my papers. "Excellent," he said, and moved on.

Finally we were put back on the train. We traveled another day and night and in the middle of the third day we arrived at our destination, a city called Weimar. And so, we were there, in the heart of the darkness, in the country that had spawned all that hatred, all that evil. I was beyond terror, though. What could be worse than what I'd already seen?

ELEVEN

WE WERE TAKEN TO a large gymnasium and made to stand while we were examined by the local people. No one seemed to want me. My German was still not that good, but I understood enough to gather that most of the people there were farmers and that they wanted strong, big girls. I suppose I looked too small and weak. Finally, a farmer did take me although I was not his first choice—I was, in fact, the only girl left. He was huge and fat, with red blotchy skin and small beady eyes. He had driven to the town on his bicycle (he was so big I couldn't figure out how it held him) and I was forced to trot after him all the way to the farm. And it was a long way, at least five miles. We passed through a very small town just before we reached his home. I was nervous, of course, wondering what lay in store for me, how I'd be treated. All the way there he snapped at me to run faster, and muttered to himself about stupid Poles. The farmhouse was huge—I was very surprised. It was a mansion compared to most farms in Poland, which were not much more than shacks or huts.

"This way," he shouted at me, leading me into the kitchen.

"Wipe your shoes!" Those were the first words his wife spoke to me. I couldn't believe my eyes when I saw her. She must have been at least four hundred pounds. I could barely see her face there was so much fat around it, so many chins. She snarled at me. "Filthy Pole." Not a good beginning.

Four children sat at the kitchen table doing homework. They looked to be from the ages of six to twelve. I gazed at them bitterly. Why could they sit there, safe and secure, when my little Moishe and my little Sarah were dead? And who knew if Yehuda and Fanny were still alive? I swallowed hard and forced myself not to cry. I couldn't give myself away.

The house was huge with so many rooms I couldn't count them. The farmer motioned me to follow him up the stairs where he showed me my room. It was just big enough for a bed and a chest of drawers but at least I'd sleep alone and I wouldn't have to worry about talking or crying out in Yiddish. I was thankful for that.

The farmer's name was Kreusz. "Hurry up," he shouted at me. I couldn't understand why he was shouting. What had I done? I followed him out to the farmyard and he pointed to the pigsty. Then he pointed to a manure pit about fifty yards away. "Your job," he yelled. "Take out the manure, put it there." He used his hands to mimic the action, in case I didn't understand. He gestured toward a shovel. I nodded my head, indicating that I understood. I glanced around quickly. There were others working. Someone was weeding the garden.

Another was over in a hutch that looked like it might have rabbits in it. And I could see activity in the barn.

"Hurry up!" he hollered throwing his hands up. "Work."

I grabbed the shovel and moved toward the pigsty. The pigs were bigger than I expected and they didn't look too friendly. My first reaction was fear, but then I stopped myself, realizing how silly that reaction was. Before the war, I was afraid of anything new or strange. But after all I'd been through, how could such a little thing scare me? An SS guard was scary; a pig wasn't, not even a large pig. I marched into the sty, shovel ready.

It was very hard work and together with the trip, the fact that I'd barely eaten in days, and the five-mile run, by the time dinner was called I could hardly stand. I was told in a nasty tone to wash up at a trough just outside the back door. My shoes were covered in manure so I took them off and rinsed them with a hose, leaving them outside. There were two tables set up in the dining room. One was covered with a white linen tablecloth and set with fine china; the other had a cotton cloth but still had a set of matching dishes. This was not at all like our farms in Poland where the farmers were peasants and the living was rough. The family's table had salami, bread, butter, and cheese. All the Polish workers sat at the other table. There were three besides me. I noticed that one of the others was allowed to sit at the family table. I found out later that she was a German girl doing her mandatory year, working for the state on a farm.

The family said their prayers, then passed the food around. One of the Poles, a man in his thirties, whispered to me, "That food isn't for us. We are only fed the skimmed-milk cheese, there, which, by the way, is always off." I suppose I should have been upset but at that moment I was so hungry I didn't care as long as I could eat something. I gobbled down the cheese, was allowed as much bread as I wanted, and drank a glass of milk.

Herr Kreusz cleared his throat and picked up a newspaper.

"This was in today's paper," he said. Then he glanced at all of us at the far table. He read slowly and very loudly, so I was able to understand almost all of it, although when he was finished I was sorry about that. I would rather not have understood.

"'German people, never forget that the atrocities of the Poles compelled the Führer to protect our German people by force! . . . The civility of the Poles to their German employers merely hides their cunning, their friendly behavior hides their deceit. . . . Germans! The Pole must never be your comrade! He is inferior to each German comrade on his farm or in his factory. Be just as Germans have always been, but never forget that you are a member of the master race!'"

He stared pointedly at me. "You are new here. But I hope you understand from the beginning your place. You will work hard, never complain, that's all."

As soon as dinner was over Herr Kreusz singled me out to follow him. We went to the barn and he pointed to the cows. I stared at him, having no idea what he wanted. "Go on," he yelled. I had no idea what he meant me to do. He made a motion with his hands and I realized he wanted me to milk them.

I shrugged my shoulders. "I don't know how," I said.

"Stupid swine," he barked at me. "You'd better learn fast."

He spit it out with such venom that I felt as if he'd slapped me.

I sat down on a stool by one of the cows, but I was so unnerved by his vicious attitude, I found it hard to concentrate as he showed me what to do. My hands wouldn't work properly at all. "Ach," he lamented, "you are all idiots, you Poles. What kind of help are you to me? What kind of workers do they give me? You're more trouble than you're worth."

I tried to get the motion right but it was so difficult with him standing over me, cursing and swearing about how stupid I was. Suddenly he caught me on the side of my head with his open hand. "Idiot!" he shrieked. "You'll curdle their milk if you keep on that way."

Every time he screamed I cringed inside. It was horrible. I couldn't understand what I'd done to deserve such a violent response. Finally he pushed me away and finished the milking himself.

"You watch me now," he ordered. "Tomorrow

morning you'll do this again, but you'd better do it right."

When he was finished he motioned me to follow him. He took me up to my room and locked me in for the night. Well, I wasn't sorry to have the door locked. I didn't like the look of one of the Poles who had been sitting beside me. He'd leered at me. The other two appeared to be much nicer. One was a big girl, a few years older than me, with pink cheeks and a cheerful smile. The other was a woman in her twenties who certainly didn't look like a farmworker. She had been quiet at dinner. The German girl had been lively and chattered away to her hosts about this and that.

First thing in the morning, I was taken out to the cows again. *Surely one of the others could do this,* I thought. *Why me?* Again, the same thing happened. He yelled and screamed at me. This time I managed to get some milk out of the cow, but not much. "Stupid swine," he shouted at me.

Reluctantly he let me go in for breakfast and then he put me to work in the rabbit hutch, cleaning the straw of the little rabbit pellets. That was horrible work as it was almost impossible to get the straw clean. In the afternoon, when I was ready to drop, the German girl approached me. She held out her hand to shake mine. "My name is Helga. Want to come into town with me?"

For a moment I was so flabbergasted I couldn't speak. Go into town? Like a free person? Of course I wore a *P* on my shirt to mark me as a Polish worker, but obviously a *P* was not the same as wearing a Star of David.

"Yes," I said uncertainly, "I'd love to. But, is it all right? Am I allowed?"

She grinned. "Of course you are. If you're with me."

She spoke in German, I spoke Polish, but she seemed to understand me perfectly.

"But that piece Herr Kreusz read yesterday," I said. "Are you allowed to be with a Pole?"

"I can't stand his bratty children," she confided in me. "They're a horrible family. What am I supposed to do here for a year with no young people my age?" She wrinkled her nose. "I'll do what I like. They can't stop me."

"Will you teach me to speak German properly?" I asked Helga.

"Certainly," she agreed without a moment's hesitation.

"Sophie over there already speaks very well." She pointed to the older woman working in the vegetable garden. "Helene"—she pointed to the big cheerful girl who was cleaning the pigsty—"will never quite catch on I'm afraid. Jerzy"—she pointed to the man who was splitting wood—"isn't interested. He's interested in other things."

"Yes," I said, "I could see that right away."

"You know," she said, gazing at me with admiration, "you could be a German girl. Look at you. You're so pretty, absolutely the Aryan ideal. What a shame you're a Slav. If you were a German you would be treated with such respect. A producer of beautiful German babies."

For a split second I swelled with pride at the compliments. For a moment I *was* a perfect German girl, ruler of the universe. A shudder passed through me.

"What is it?" she asked, concerned.

"Nothing," I said. But how easy it was to be seduced. For a moment, even after what they had put me through, I could feel the magic of that dream. How tempting to be better than everyone else in the entire world. Better, smarter, prettier, entitled to all the good things. Oh yes, how tempting.

TWELVE

HELENE, THE BIG Polish girl, was hanged in August. In September I knew I had to escape Herr Kreusz or I, too, would be killed. Somehow he'd find a way.

The first few months I was at the farm consisted of Herr Kreusz's unrelenting cruelty, broken only by Helga's occasional kindness. I don't know what I had expected. I suppose when I was in Poland, I really hadn't thought that far ahead. All I was concerned with was survival—living one more day. I naturally assumed I would be treated badly by the Germans, just not as badly as I was. Herr Kreusz never spoke to me. He yelled. He screamed. He hit me. He kicked me. I never had a moment's peace. Even his children followed his lead—every time I walked past the six-year-old he would hit me or kick me.

But in my spare time Helga worked with me on my German until by early fall I spoke flawlessly, with no accent at all. It surprised Helga. Slavs were supposed to be stupid. She couldn't quite understand it.

Helene spent all her spare time with the young men from the other farms, sometimes with German boys who were home on leave. One day Herr Kreusz discovered her in the barn with Peter, a German boy from the nearby town. Without hesitation he called the local police and reported them both. Peter had his head shaved and was marched through the town to humiliate him. Helene was hanged, the punishment for being intimate with a German of pure blood.

I hadn't gotten to know her well, but I'd liked her. She was a peasant girl, full of dirty jokes, good humor, and a lust for living. She screamed and screamed and begged them to spare her life as they dragged her off to be hanged.

After that incident Herr Kreusz seemed to focus his hatred more and more on me. I thought that one day he would either kill me by beating me to death, or make up something I'd done so the authorities would hang me for him. I confided my worries to Helga one evening after dinner as we sat outside on the woodpile.

"You should run away," she suggested.

I just laughed. "Run away? They'd catch me. Then they'd have a good reason to hang me, too."

"Two other girls who were here before you ran away."

"What?"

"It's true."

"But why didn't you tell me before?"

"I don't want you to go. I'll only be here another month. Can't you stay one more month?"

"In one more month I could be dead," I said. Gingerly I touched my chin where he'd belted me only that morning. It was swollen and tender. "And even when he doesn't hit me," I continued, "he screams constantly and it's horrible. No one has ever screamed at me before," I said softly.

"What?" she sounded amazed. "That couldn't be possible."

"Why? Because all Poles are brutish?" I asked her. "Well, it's not true. They aren't. I'm not used to it."

"I'll tell you what," she said. "I'm going into Weimar next week. Would you like me to take a letter for you to the employment office? Ask if they will find you a different farm? They know the problem with Herr Kreusz. Maybe they will."

"Would you?"

"I offered, didn't I?"

She took my letter. Nothing happened for weeks. Finally, it was time for Helga to return home. I was terrified of being left on the farm with no one to turn to. But the day after Helga left, Herr Kreusz came stomping over to me and slapped me across the face.

"That's the gratitude you show!" he shrieked. "Asking to be moved. Just before the harvest, too!" He slapped me again so hard I fell backward into the pigsty. "That's where you belong. In the filth with the pigs. Go! Now!"

"What do you mean?"

"Pack your things. Go to the office in Weimar. They are moving you." And he stalked away.

I cleaned myself as best as I could, threw my

clothes into a bag and began the long walk into Weimar.

When I arrived at the office, late in the day, the man in charge looked me over, noting my bruised and swollen face.

"There's a new batch coming in today," he said briskly. "I think you've been with Herr Kreusz long enough. I'm sending you to a lovely family. Herr Reymann was just in yesterday looking for someone. The girl who brought your letter told me that you wanted to wait to leave until she, too, left the farm. Has she gone?"

"Yes," I said. I wasn't surprised that Helga had done that. I wasn't *really* an equal, after all. More like a pet dog. And she hadn't finished with me when I wanted to leave.

"Sit and wait there. I'll let Herr Reymann know you are here."

About an hour later Herr Reymann arrived. He was driving a car. Only very important people were allowed fuel for cars. I wondered who he was exactly.

His farm was a huge mass of land, perfectly kept. His house was much finer than the Kreuszes'. He had three children, ages ten, twelve, and fourteen. His wife was a neat, precise woman. I washed up before dinner, and then I was seated at the long dining room table with two other Poles, two men in their twenties. We all sat at the same table as the family. I wondered why he wasn't worried about being arrested. Poles were never supposed to eat at the same table as Germans. Frau Reymann offered me bread. We ate a delicious vegetable stew and drank buttermilk—everyone ate the same food, the Polish workers and the family. In fact, they encouraged me to have seconds. I couldn't believe my luck. I had obviously landed with a cultured and kind family. I was thrilled!

"Maria," said Frau Reymann, "in the mornings you can clean inside the house. In the afternoons you'll help in the field."

"That will be fine," I answered in German.

"My," she remarked, "your German is excellent. You know," she said proudly, "Herr Reymann is a very important official of the Nazi Party so we must always keep our house in perfect condition. He often has senior members coming here for meetings. I'm sure you'll do a good job and you'll work hard."

I swallowed, then answered calmly. "I'll work very hard for you," I assured her.

A Nazi official. *Now,* I thought, *I really am in the belly of the beast.* And only moments before I had been so excited.

After dinner the children gathered to play a board game. They were cheerful children, polite and relaxed. The fourteen-year-old girl, Charlotte, seemed to take a liking to me.

"You can watch," she offered.

Obviously I couldn't play with them—I was a Pole. And Germans mustn't ever treat Poles as equals. But, from her point of view, she was being nice, asking me to watch.

"Yes, I'd like that very much."

The children set up the board, and each took a piece to move.

"What is it called?" I asked.

"Jews Out," Charlotte answered. "You see, the first one to get the most Jews out of town wins."

"Oh," I said, the food I'd just eaten suddenly churning in my stomach. I hoped I wouldn't be sick.

The ten-year-old, Christian, smiled at me. He had big blue eyes, and blond hair that fell over his face in an unruly way.

"Our uncle Wolfgang, he has led troops into your country," Christian said. "He has gotten rid of thousands of Jews. Maybe *ten* thousand!"

I started to find it hard to breathe.

"Really? You must be proud of him," I said, but my voice cracked.

"Oh we are," agreed the twelve-year-old, Hans. With his short brown hair and brown eyes, he wasn't as perfect looking as Christian.

"Would you like to see some pictures?"

Before I could answer he ran over to the hutch by the dining room table and brought back a pile of photos.

"He sent us these from Poland," Hans beamed. "He takes his camera everywhere and always sends us pictures." He handed them to me.

I wondered what the pictures would be. Perhaps his uncle standing proudly in front of bombed Polish ruins. I really didn't want to look but I couldn't refuse. Still, I never expected what I saw. At first, I couldn't even understand what I was looking at: German soldiers, their guns aimed at naked men, women, and children, standing over a large pit; a naked woman, holding a small child against her chest, a soldier aiming at her; a long shot of a deep pit full of dead bodies—I stopped looking. Mute, I handed them back to Hans. He didn't even notice my distress.

"See," he said proudly, "I wasn't making it up. Father has an important job, too, though. It is equally important, you know, to produce food for Germany. That's why he stays on the farm and does his Party work from here."

The children began to play.

"I've almost got that slimy Jew out," Charlotte said, tossing her long blond braid. "I *always* beat the boys."

"Maybe," said Hans. "But soon I'll be old enough to go fight and then I can do the real thing like Uncle Wolfgang. I can pull the Jews' beards, the old ones, and cut them off and make them crawl on the ground and pray. As if God would listen to them! He'd as soon listen to a rat pray." He turned to me. "I saw Herr Kreusz do that to the old Jews in town. Anyone could do it if they wanted. But the fun was over too soon and now they're all gone."

"The war will be over before you're old enough," scoffed Christian. "We'll rule the whole world then." He looked at me. "Don't worry. You'll be better off with us in charge. I'm sure you'll live better here than you ever could in Poland. At school we learned that you Poles live in the worst . . ." He searched for a word.

"Squalor." Charlotte helped him out.

"Yes, squalor. And you don't go to school. No one is educated."

Very quietly I said, "We had many universities and we all went to school before the Germans came."

They look at me, shocked.

"That can't be," objected Hans. "You are just making it up." He seemed very upset. His father and mother sat on the other side of the room so they hadn't heard me.

"You're right, of course," I conceded. "I'm sorry. I didn't mean to upset you. I only *dreamed* that it might be like that."

"You can dream, of course," Charlotte commented. "Even a Pole can dream. One out!" she declared. "I'm going for Levin next. You two had better get moving."

I sat down and watched as they methodically got rid of each Jew and every Jewish shop on the board. I couldn't understand the world I lived in. It felt like a type of dream where nothing made sense. The children seemed so nice. Their parents, too. They were the kind of people who would probably never cheat or lie or steal. They were "good" people. And yet they could murder, or condone murder, with no problem. I had to conclude then that they saw Jews as not even human. They had to believe in that lie so deeply that murder was no longer murder; torture and cruelty no longer held the same meaning. I wondered if they *really* saw us as lower than animals. I decided to try to find out.

"I saw an old dog as we came here," I said. "It looked mean."

They glanced up at me.

"Should that dog be killed, do you think?"

"Oh yes," said Hans. "It must be put down immediately or it could harm us."

That must be how they view Jews, I thought.

"I knew a boy who used to torture dogs, then kill them."

Charlotte appeared shocked. "What a *horrible* boy he must have been. You Poles really have no moral sense, do you? Why, anyone with any decency would put an animal to death painlessly. It's just a poor, dumb creature."

It had to go beyond hate, I thought, *didn't it, because they'd treat a rabid dog better than a Jew?*

"I tried to stop him."

"Good for you," said Charlotte. "Now that you are here, you must concentrate on those good traits."

"I will," I assured her.

"I think Maria should go to her room now, children. She has a busy day tomorrow," said Frau Reymann.

"Yes, Frau Reymann," I responded. "I would like that very much."

Once in my room I sat on the bed, staring straight ahead. I would have given the world to be with Shmuel right then, or Fanny or Yehuda. Why had I ever agreed to do this? I was all alone among people who hated me.

I'd rather be dead, I thought. *I'd rather be dead.*

THIRTEEN

WITHIN WEEKS OF ARRIVING at the Reymanns' all I could think about was killing myself. I hated everybody and everything. The nicer the Reymanns were to me the more I hated them. My only pleasure was in deceiving them.

They had no inkling of this, however. In fact, my duties quickly expanded to helping Frau Reymann with the children because they found me to be polite, smart, and efficient.

One day, I was sitting with Charlotte quizzing her on her geography, when an idea hit me. We were going over the cities in Germany. Before I had time to think about it, I spoke.

"You know," I suggested casually, "my great-grandparents came from Berlin."

She looked at me, stunned.

"Do you mean you aren't a Pole?"

"Well, of course I am *now*. But I do have *some* German Aryan blood in me."

"That explains it!" she exclaimed. "You're so cultured and well spoken. And you're so beautiful!"

"My parents died in a house fire," I said, "and all our documents were burned with them. My grandmother and I were out shopping. That's why I survived. The Germans couldn't give me any special treatment. After all, we had no proof." I lowered my voice. "Frankly, I don't blame them. You have to be careful not to mix the bloodlines. And my grandmother did marry a Pole. But my mother met and married a German boy, so you see I have quite a lot of Aryan blood in me." I allowed a tear to trickle down my face.

"Oh, you poor dear!" Charlotte began to weep as well. "So close. *Almost* one of us, but doomed to be forever on the outside. Still, maybe Father can help you. He's so important he can do anything!"

I smiled to myself. *Stupid Jew? Maybe not so stupid. What would Charlotte do, I wondered, if I told her right then that I was a Jew? Would I have changed in front of her very eyes? Would I have gone from beautiful and smart to evil in one second? Yes, I would have. I suddenly would have become a carrier of disease, and even though I seemed nice, obviously I would have been plotting against them. I suddenly would have become evil inside, rotten. Well, I could be what they wanted me to be. Couldn't I?*

At dinner Charlotte encouraged me to tell my story to her father. "I can't," I protested, pretending to hold back tears. "*You* tell it, Charlotte. It's too hard for me."

Charlotte told my story with enthusiasm. Frau Reymann dabbed her eyes before Charlotte was even finished.

"Heydrich," she said to her husband, "you must help this child. She speaks perfect German, look at her.

She needn't be treated like the other Poles. She's part Aryan, isn't she?"

"You're correct," he agreed. "Charlotte, why not take her to your meeting tonight?"

"Could I?"

"Tell them I have ordered it. You need help carrying all the refreshments we are supplying tonight, don't you?"

"Yes, Father." Charlotte smiled, clapping her hands together in glee. She turned to me. "It's called the League of German Maidens. I've just graduated to it from Young Maidens because I'm fourteen now. Wait, I'll go get into my uniform!" She returned in a full blue skirt, a crisp white blouse, and a cotton neckerchief clasped with a wooden ring. On her feet were heavy marching shoes.

"Oh, don't worry," she said, smiling, as she saw me looking at her shoes, "no marching today. Today we're having a lecture on our role as women in the Third Reich."

We were allowed to ride bicycles into town, our carriers full of treats from the farm—apples fresh off the trees, buns, and real butter.

"It's only a small group," Charlotte chattered as we rode. "Mostly children of the farmers in the area. Once a month, though, we meet with the larger group in Weimar. It's in a wonderful old building in Weimar—it used to be a synagogue, actually."

We arrived and Charlotte hurried ahead of me, as I was carrying all the food, which was very heavy. I hoped that my story would improve my situation a bit; perhaps the family wouldn't look down on me quite so much. But I was still a servant, of course. My blood wasn't pure enough for anything else. I struggled after Charlotte with the bags into a small dry goods store.

"We meet in the back," she said. I followed her into a room where the other girls were already sitting down getting ready to listen to a speaker.

"That's our leader," Charlotte explained. She went over to her and pointed at me. Their leader nodded and replied. Charlotte hurried back to me. "She said you may stand at the back of the room."

When everyone was settled the leader began her talk. "Girls," she announced, "the focus of today's meeting has been changed slightly. We will, of course, still discuss how woman can best serve the Reich. But one of the ways is charity and doing charitable works. Girls, I am speaking of war relief. Now, I know you are all very busy with school and your duties here, but I will need you to become busier still. Clothes are pouring in from our conquered neighbors, especially Poland, and they need attention. They have already been sewn and fixed at factories run by the lesser people, like the Poles." At this point she stopped to glare at me. "But their work is so shabby. Before they are distributed you must take time, voluntarily, to come in and check through the piles. Any loose buttons or hems are to be fixed. No one in our Reich will go hungry or cold this winter, but we must help."

My knees began to buckle beneath me. The familiar dizziness came over me. Those pictures Hans had shown me—the victims naked . . . I had thought it was pure cruelty, strictly for the purpose of humiliation. But then I saw that the Germans were far too practical for their cruelty not to also have some functional use. Those were the clothes of murdered Jews, Poles, and Russians. Perhaps Mama and Moishe and Sarah had been forced to undress before they'd been shot.

I sank to the floor and put my head between my knees. Everyone was so caught up in her speech that no one noticed.

She talked on and on. She lectured the girls on their duty to bring as many children as possible into the Reich, to bear pure Aryan children, *lots* of them. And then she ended on another note.

"Girls, each time we meet we talk about the Jews. I am happy to tell you that I have been told that Germany will soon be Jew-free. All of Germany. For inspiration I will read to you from one of our Führer's greatest speeches, given in the Parliament on January 30, 1930, and published for our enlightenment:

> DURING THE TIMES OF MY STRUGGLE FOR POWER IT WAS IN THE FIRST INSTANCE THE JEWISH RACE WHICH RECEIVED MY PROPHECIES WITH LAUGHTER WHEN I SAID THAT I WOULD ONE DAY TAKE OVER THE LEADERSHIP OF THE STATE, AND WITH IT THAT OF THE WHOLE NATION, AND THAT I WOULD THEN AMONG MANY OTHER THINGS SETTLE THE JEWISH

PROBLEM. THEIR LAUGHTER WAS UPROARIOUS, BUT I THINK FOR SOME TIME NOW THEY HAVE BEEN LAUGHING ON THE OTHER SIDE OF THEIR FACE. TODAY I WILL ONCE MORE BE A PROPHET: IF THE INTERNATIONAL JEWISH FINANCIERS IN AND OUTSIDE EUROPE SHOULD SUCCEED IN PLUNGING THE NATIONS ONCE MORE INTO A WORLD WAR, THEN THE RESULT WILL NOT BE THE BOLSHEVISATION OF THE EARTH, AND THUS THE VICTORY OF JEWRY, BUT THE ANNIHILATION OF THE JEWISH RACE IN EUROPE."

Why, I thought to myself, *did none of the adults listening take him seriously? Did they believe he could never take power? That the German people would never back him? Well, they were wrong. And we were paying for their blindness.*

My dizziness passed, so I stood up and tried to look cheerful as Charlotte, smiling, came over to me.

"Come on," she said, "we'll sort the clothes and then we can have our snack."

"Why don't I lay the snacks out on the table," I suggested, "so they'll be ready when you're finished?"

"Good idea," she said, beaming, then moved over to a large pile of clothes.

I couldn't have put my hands on those clothes, even if it meant I would have been discovered at that very moment. Nothing would have made me touch them.

On the way home I could bear Charlotte's blindness and brainwashing no longer. Pretending to be completely ignorant, I asked her, "Charlotte, please explain something to me."

"Certainly," she agreed, delighted to be asked.

"Many German Jews have lived here for over a thousand years, correct?"

"Yes, as I'm told."

"Why is it that only *now* they pose such a threat to your country?"

"Oh, but they *always* did."

"But, I still don't understand. Isn't Germany the greatest civilization in the world?"

"Yes," she agreed proudly.

"With the best writers, composers, philosophers, architects, everything?"

"Yes!"

"How could Germany develop like that if the Jews were so evil and so smart? Surely over the course of a thousand years they would have *ruined* your country. I mean, that's what evil people do. They destroy. And yet, Germany grew and flourished."

There was a long pause. For a moment, I think she was so confused she couldn't answer.

"Well," she said finally, "I don't know. But they must have been kept in check somehow."

"Sometimes," I said, "there were laws passed against them. But often Jews were members of German society."

She started to pedal very hard.

"Why do you know so much about them?" she asked suspiciously.

"Oh," I replied, trying to keep my tone of voice casual, "our priest has told us how evil and clever they are. But he wasn't too clever himself and he could never *really* explain to me *how* they are dangerous. For instance, if it is true that they run the banks, why would they want to be Bolsheviks? Bolsheviks are Communists, and I can tell you the first thing Communists do when in power is take over all the banks."

"Are you criticizing what our Führer said?" Charlotte accused me, her voice filled with outrage.

"No! No! I'm so stupid I don't understand it. Please, please explain. It makes my head hurt."

There was another pause. "It's like this," Charlotte said slowly, obviously trying to work it out in her own head. "The Aryan race is the top race, the most advanced. I'm afraid that you Russians and Poles are the bottom race. But Jews, they are not even *of* the human race. They are really like a deadly bacteria that can infect an entire country and kill it. Somehow, I suppose, Germany has kept the disease in check—but suddenly it threatened to overwhelm us. Would you hesitate to kill a bad germ by dousing it with disinfectant to save your body?"

"No," I answered. It sounded like she was reciting a lesson she had been taught.

"Of course not! And we must treat the Jew the same way. It isn't murder to get rid of the Jew. It is a cleansing, like killing rats who only breed disease."

There was a silence, then, because I couldn't find my voice. Her words left me not angry, but with an overpowering sense of hopelessness. *They* will *succeed in wiping us out,* I thought, *each and every one of us. And the few like me who might survive—what would be left of our Jewishness? Nothing. The Jewish New Year would soon arrive, the holiest of holidays, and I would have to pretend it didn't exist. Was I still a Jew if I couldn't be a Jew?*

"Maria," Charlotte asked, "do you understand now?"

"Yes," I replied. "Thank you, Charlotte. I *do* understand. Finally. It's true that Germans are superior, because only you could explain it to me."

FOURTEEN

SHMUEL HAD INSTRUCTED ME to keep love in my heart, not hate. I recited the Shehecheyanu every night as I'd promised, but it didn't help. I *wasn't* happy to have reached this day, or thankful. I was bitter that I was still alive and about all that I had seen. And if there was any love left in my heart I couldn't find it. I'd become cynical and manipulative. And I was a liar. I pretended constantly to be someone I was not and the more I pretended the more I hated myself.

I started thinking of all the ways I could kill myself. Rat poison was one possibility. *That would be appropriate,* I thought. *And I could leave a note, declaring myself a Jew, a rat, who had to be eliminated.* Or, I considered taking Herr Reymann's shotgun and blowing my head off. But that would've been very messy. Still, what did I care if the children saw it? If they had known who I really was, they'd be glad to see me dead. Or, there was hanging. I liked that idea the best. No blood. No mess. I could do it in the barn, climb up on a stool, then kick—a few minutes of agony, and I'd be dead.

I couldn't really think of a good reason not to do

it. I was constantly thinking *maybe tomorrow, maybe tonight.*

The winter was very mild and after the hard work of harvest there was lots of time to think of things like that. I milked the cows in the morning—Charlotte had taught me how to do it properly—and during the day I helped prepare meals, cleaned, helped the children with their homework, supervised them after supper. It was work, but no harder than what I was used to at home. Because of my status as part German, Herr Reymann allowed me the use of his library. If I died, by my own hand or another's, at least I wouldn't die stupid. If I lived, I still wanted to be a scholar, so I went to bed as early as I could and I read. They had electricity there, not like the farms in Poland, and I had a small lamp by my bed.

I came to one conclusion and it unsettled me a little in my quest to be a scholar. I could see from my reading that German society was very developed intellectually. And yet, from what the children had told me, the intellectuals had by and large supported Hitler. So my conclusion was this—a person, the world, needed *heart* more than intellect. And I understood that my problems, my misery, stemmed from the same place—my intellect was big, but my heart was empty.

I'd been at the Reymanns' for a month when I suddenly spiked a very high fever. I was sick but I couldn't let on that I was sick. I had been told by the doctors when we first got to Germany that any worker who couldn't work would be sent back to

Poland. For a real Polish worker it would be wonderful. For me, it would be a death sentence. And although I was seriously thinking about dying, I didn't want to die that way. So I had to pretend that I wasn't sick. Every chance I got, I ran to the sink and splashed cold water on my face in an attempt to bring down my fever. I did my chores, sat with the children, forced myself to eat, even if I couldn't keep it down. After two days Frau Reymann noticed something was wrong—by then I was so ill I could barely stand. All I would admit to was a slight cold. She fussed and made me go to bed and had Charlotte bring me hot drinks. I couldn't understand it. I was a Pole. Why did she care? Or maybe she didn't care. Maybe she would have to prove to the authorities that I'd been bedridden and useless for two weeks before she could send me back and that was why she was making me stay in bed. She was a Nazi, after all. How could I possibly think she cared about a stupid Pole? So after two days in bed, even though I was weak and still had a slight fever, I forced myself out of bed and made sure I ate dinner with the family I declared myself to be completely recovered. The two Polish workers picked that night to invite me to go to the local pub with them. As much to prove that I was well to Frau Reymann as anything else, I said, "Yes, of course, I'd love to," before she could object.

Their names were Anton and Tadeusz. As we walked, Anton asked me how I was feeling. "Awful," I admitted, without thinking.

"But why not stay in bed?" he asked, bewildered. "Maybe they'll send you home!"

I was feeling so woozy, my legs were so weak, I was chilled—I couldn't think straight. Why had I said that? How could I explain myself? If either of them found out I was Jewish they'd probably turn me in. I certainly couldn't take a chance that they might not hate Jews.

I had to think of something fast. "We had nothing in Poland," I said. "I was starving. At least here I can eat."

"No sweetheart to go home to?" Tadeusz asked.

"I'm too young for that," I scoffed.

They looked at each other and smiled approvingly. They seemed happy with that answer.

"Tell us where home is," Anton said.

"Zloczow," I replied.

Anton slapped his thigh and said, "But so am I! We must know some of the same people. Which area did you live in? What street?"

"No, no, you mistake me," I said quickly, breaking out into more of a sweat than I was already in. "I was born in Zloczow but we moved when I was very young to Lvov. So I can't remember much. I must have been three or four when we moved. I remember the castle, though," I added, to sound more convincing. "I loved the castle."

"Everyone loves that old castle," Anton agreed.

"Do you miss your families?" I asked, to change the subject.

"Yes," they both answered together. Both were

married. Tadeusz had two small children. Anton had left his new bride at home. "Although," he added, "she got a notice recently. She may soon have to come to work in Germany, too."

They seemed to accept my story, but I felt faint by the time we reached the pub. That had been a very close call. From then on we were friendly to each other and I could see that they watched out for me, never quite trusting the Germans, as big brothers would. Still, I never told them my secret.

About a week after I'd finally recovered, Charlotte took me with her to a youth rally in Weimar. Her entire League of German Maidens group—or BDM, as they called it—was going, and Herr Reymann decided that I should go, too, as a kind of servant/companion. Hans and Christian were also attending as part of the Jungvolk, but they'd be with another group.

We all met in the town and then we were driven into Weimar on a bus. There we were billeted in different houses. Charlotte, a girl called Rosa, and I were housed with an elderly couple who were very nice. I, of course, slept on a mat on the floor in between the two small beds the girls slept in. First thing in the morning a bus picked us up and took us to a stadium. Charlotte was going to compete in races and gymnastics later in the day but first there was an elaborate ceremony. We sat up in the stands with the rest of the group as about ten different bands marched in, each group dressed in a slightly different military uniform, each group playing an inspiring war melody. One group, called The Drums, was so compelling that even I was carried away by their playing. Their drums were long, reaching all the way from their waists to their knees, and the sound that came out of them was deep and vibrated right through you. It was mysterious and dangerous and somehow primitive. It was unsettling. "The drummers are to remind us of the boys who went into battle in the olden days," Charlotte explained. "It's said that they drummed until they died."

"How noble!" sighed Rosa.

How stupid! I thought. *What's noble about being killed in a war?*

After the drummers left the Jungvolk came in, all dressed in black and white. They marched themselves into a huge swastika on the floor of the arena. Then the Jungmädel followed them, dressed all in white, and they formed a big circle around the boys. The bands began to play together, and the drummers drummed; it was quite a spectacle. The girls clapped their hands in glee. Then it was their turn. Charlotte made her way to an area on the floor where the gym was set up. She proceeded to do all kinds of things over the horse: flips, somersaults, even back flips. I must say I was impressed. In the end she won a silver medal.

Finally, the boys formed another swastika. A Hitler Youth leader made a speech, but the sound was bad and I couldn't quite make out what he was saying. All the thousands of children replied when he raised his arm and yelled, "Adolf Hitler." They screamed back, *"Sieg Heil! Sieg Heil! Sieg Heil!* Hail Victory!"

The stadium shook. The sound rattled through me, overwhelming me. *"How can they lose?"* I thought. *This regime will last one thousand years, just like Hitler promised. And all the Jews will, eventually, die.* My thoughts of suicide returned stronger than ever. I resolved to do something about it the very next day, feeling utterly and completely hopeless.

We hurried out of the stadium and tried to find our bus. Hundreds of them were crammed into a large field and a paved lot by the stadium. There was chaos as the different groups tried to find their buses.

Our bus was near a stand of trees; Rosa pointed out where we were to go. We walked there with some Hitler Youth, boys the same age as Charlotte's group, fourteen to eighteen. Just as we got to our buses a huge gang of kids of around the same age scrambled out from behind the trees and began pelting us with small rocks and stones. "Puppets!" they yelled. "Black boots!" And I couldn't catch much else because soon the boys of the Hitler Youth were in an all-out fight with the other group. The girls screamed and ran into the buses but not Charlotte for some reason. She seemed frozen. I grabbed her hand and tried to pull her away from the melee when a tall young man suddenly tumbled into us, having been shoved by one of the Hitler Youth. Charlotte screamed, "Get off me you oaf. Get off me!" He did try to scramble out of her way because she seemed to have conquered her initial shock and was punching and kicking him.

"Charlotte?" he said, catching her fists in his hands.

She looked up at him. "Georg?"

"Yes!"

"But, but what are you doing?" she said. "Are you crazy?"

"Charlotte, it's so wonderful to see you. When do you leave Weimar?"

"Tomorrow at noon."

"Meet me for breakfast at the old café on Goethestrasse, all right?"

"I can't," Charlotte said.

"I'll be there," he replied, then ran off to beat up another Hitler Youth.

I couldn't believe what I'd just heard. Charlotte grabbed my hand and pulled me into the bus.

"Not a word," she whispered.

"Who is he?"

"A friend from school," she said. "Or, that is until he stopped school last year. You see, boys or girls who aren't going on to University stop school here at fourteen and will usually apprentice or something."

She babbled on about the school system in Germany but I could tell that wasn't what she was thinking about.

"Father, of course, wants me to continue until I've finished high school but I doubt I can go to

University." I actually heard a note of regret in her voice.

"Why not?" I asked. "You're so clever. Your marks are almost perfect."

"German girls aren't supposed to learn," she said. "Remember that speech our leader gave? I'll be expected to marry. Intellectuals are not well thought of," she explained. "They're just troublemakers. But if I finish high school, perhaps I can teach sports. I'd like that."

All that time she'd been staring out the window of the bus, watching the ruckus outside, talking as if to convince me that she really didn't care about what was going on. Or convince herself. Adults began to arrive and finally they scared off the large groups of teenagers. Soon after that our bus pulled away.

"What was all that about?" I asked. I couldn't believe what had just happened. Everything I'd seen in Germany had been so orderly, so controlled.

"They call themselves the Pirates," Charlotte replied, and her voice was scornful. "They're just a bunch of hooligans. They like to beat up Hitler Youth boys whenever they can."

"And Georg? Are you going to meet him?"

"Of course not! But I do have some errands to run in the morning. So you wait at the house and I'll meet you back there before our bus comes."

I knew she was lying. And that was the moment I saw her, for the first time, as a human being. She liked that boy. She liked him very much. And she was going to sneak off and meet him for breakfast.

That night, as I lay on the hard mat on the cold floor, I experienced a moment of hope. My despair lifted, not altogether, but slightly, because there was actually a group of children who were not for Hitler—right there in Weimar. And somehow they weren't in jail or in concentration camps; and they had avoided being part of the huge Nazi system. It wasn't much, but it was a small crack in the perfect machine.

After that outing, when we returned to the farm, I noticed a marked changed in Charlotte's behavior. She started going out for a long walk every night right after dinner. Of course it was dark then but she told her parents that it was part of a new training program for her group. A couple of times I heard her sneaking out of her room, later, after everyone was asleep. There was no doubt in my mind that she was meeting Georg. Her entire demeanor showed that she had fallen deeply in love. She was in an anxious, agitated state almost all the time.

One night I was helping her with her homework, as usual. She always had quite a bit of work to do at home because at school at least five hours out of every day were spent in physical activity; children's physical fitness was considered much more important than anything else. Still, she had to study the usual subjects, plus biology, which included all the materials on the purity of the Aryan race, plus extra studies on race.

That night she couldn't wait to get finished but

she had three questions left to answer. She whispered to me, "Maria, please will you do my homework for me tonight? I have to go out."

I stared at her for a moment, and then I had a thought. "I'll do it for you tonight," I said, "if one night you'll take me with you when you go out."

"I couldn't!"

"Oh," I said, "I'm afraid, then, that I'm not clever enough to do your work."

"But I *have* to get out tonight," she said.

"Take me with you," I urged her. "It's so boring here for me. Please." And I was telling her the truth although what prompted me to be so rash I'll never know. Except that I was young, too, and her excitement was contagious. Suddenly I also wanted to be reckless. Me, wanting to be reckless. I couldn't help but wonder what Shmuel would think.

"All right," she agreed. "Here's my homework." And she told her parents she had finished her work and got dressed for her walk. I helped Hans and Christian, and when they were finished with their work I took Charlotte's up to my room so Frau Reymann wouldn't notice me doing it. I read it over quickly.

How can we recognize a person's race?
(1) Summarize the spiritual characteristics of three individual races.
(2) Observe people where special racial features have drawn your attention, also with respect to their bearing when moving or when speaking. Observe their expressions.

(3) WHAT STRIKES YOU ABOUT THE WAY A JEW TALKS AND SINGS?

How was I going to do this? And yet, since I'd been here I'd seen so much propaganda that, in a way, I could answer the questions. Jews were described as hunched over in their movements, their voices slimy or shrill, their gestures ugly. They were portrayed as having huge hooked noses and small beady eyes. As for spiritual characteristics, I supposed the answer had to be that Jews were sly, conniving, greedy, untrustworthy.

Slowly, methodically, I worked through the answers, paying particular attention to my grammar and spelling which was not as good written as it was spoken. It was almost as if another person were doing the work—I felt nothing. I simply concentrated on the challenge. By the time I was finished I'd painted an appropriately nasty picture of the Jew. And then I went to work on the Slavs.

FIFTEEN

THE NEXT NIGHT, after everyone was in bed, Charlotte knocked softly on my door. I followed her down the darkened hall and out through the kitchen. My heart thudded in my chest. Why had I asked her to take me? What if we were caught? I'd certainly be shipped back to Poland. Still, it was too late to turn back. She offered me Hans' bike, and we pedaled down the darkened road. There was a moon out, and stars, and the night was very mild for the end of October. Soon I was sweating from the effort of pedaling so quickly. Just outside the town was a small clearing surrounded by trees and I could see a light shining through the bare branches. We got off our bicycles and walked toward it. We hadn't said a word the entire way. When we stepped into the clearing, I saw a group of about ten boys and three girls sitting around a campfire. One of the boys had a guitar and the rest started to sing just as we arrived.

Hark the hearty fellows sing!
Strum that banjo, pluck that string!
And the lasses all join in.
We're going to get rid of Hitler,

And he can't do a thing.
Hitler's power may lay us low,
And keep us locked in chains,
But we will smash the chains one day,
We'll be free again.
We've got fists and we can fight,
We've got knives and will get them out.

Charlotte ran to Georg who obviously had been on the lookout for her and threw her arms around him. They kissed. In front of everyone! That surprised me as much as the song they were singing. Well, actually, I'm not sure what surprised me more. In fact, "surprised" is hardly the word. I was shocked. Charlotte involved with someone like this? The other young people looked at me suspiciously, at first, until Charlotte explained who I was. Then they must have realized that I couldn't give them away without giving myself away—a Polish slave shouldn't be running around the countryside. They were all dressed in fairly shabby clothes but none of them looked like they were starving. They continued to sing.

We march by banks of Ruhr and Rhine
And smash the Hitler Youth in twain.

I sank down to my knees, barely able to take in what was happening. One of the girls and a couple of boys came over to introduce themselves and talk to me. They were friendly and treated me as an equal, not as a slave. They asked me about Poland and how I thought the war had *really* started. I told them what I knew. They asked about the Russians. I told them that the Russians had been good to us. When it was time to leave, they shook hands with me. Charlotte kissed Georg good-bye and collected me and we cycled home.

"Well," I said, "you're certainly a dark horse." I paused. "Charlotte, your father is an important official. How do you think he'd react if he discovered who you were spending time with? Sneaking out with?"

"He'd be angry," she said.

"That hardly describes how he would react," I chastised her, "and you know it. He'd be furious. And rightly so. It would reflect very badly on him."

I couldn't believe I was saying this to her, but very quickly I saw the danger—not only to her but to me. After all, what if someone else caught her before her father did? Some other Nazi. They would investigate her entire family. And they'd find out that I'd gone to that gathering with Charlotte. The more I thought about it the clearer the danger became in my mind. I was glad I'd asked her to take me. I had to stop her. Stop her from participating in an anti-Nazi group. The irony was not lost on me.

"Do you believe in anything they say?" I asked her.

"Of course not!"

"Then, then, how can you be with them?"

"Oh, Maria, that must be obvious."

I sighed. "Yes, it is. But what about Georg? Isn't he in danger?"

"Not really," Charlotte told me. "After all, they

can't shoot these boys. They're German! Maybe if he was caught he'd be sent to a Youth Reform Camp. Well, he's willing to take that chance. Soon he'll be called up to the army. There's no work for him. He and his group like to spend time together."

"Beating up Hitler Youth," I remarked.

"He tried Hitler Youth. All they do is march, he says. It's unbearable."

I shrugged to myself. She wasn't making any sense but why should she? She was wild over the boy and he must have seemed dangerous and romantic.

We arrived back at the farmhouse around one in the morning. We crept into the kitchen, shutting the door softly behind us. Suddenly the overhead light flashed on. Frau Reymann stood by the light switch, staring at us. I can't describe how I felt at that moment. Sick. I felt sick. We'd been discovered and I'd certainly be returned to Poland, where my identity would be immediately discovered. And then how would I die? The pictures Hans had showed me flashed in front of me—naked by a pit . . . and then everything went black.

When I woke up I was in my bed, Frau Reymann standing over me, holding a cold cloth to my forehead. She shook her head and made a clucking sound. Charlotte hovered near the door.

"You girls are very fortunate," Frau Reymann said, "that Charlotte's father was called out late tonight to a meeting. If he'd discovered you missing . . . well, I dread to think. I'm sure you know what the consequences would be, Maria," she said sternly. "As does Charlotte. However, it was me who noticed Charlotte was not in her bed and that makes both of you very lucky. I understand that it's tempting to sneak out to a party," she said. "I was young once, too. But it must not happen again."

My breath was coming in short gasps.

"Are you feeling better now, Maria?"

I nodded, unable to speak, quite overwhelmed by our close call.

"Good." She put her hand on my forehead for a moment and then got up swiftly and left the room, shutting the door behind her.

I turned over, buried my head in my pillow, and burst out sobbing. I cried with such intensity I thought I might shake the whole house, that they'd hear me. Maybe they did. But I couldn't stop. It was the way she'd put her hand on my face. Touched me like I was a human being. And it reminded me so much of Mama, and I missed her so desperately at that moment, I felt my heart would break. Later, as my crying subsided, I thought about Frau Reymann's treatment of me when I'd been sick. Maybe it had nothing to do with sending me back to Poland. Maybe she had been genuinely concerned. Maybe she was simply a good person. *But how could that be? She was a Nazi!* That meant she was evil through and through. Didn't it? I pushed my hands against my head because I felt like my head was going to split. Why couldn't I understand the world around me? There had to be an explanation for this—but it was beyond me. Finally, the tears and the stress of the evening catching up with me, I fell into a deep sleep.

I awoke suddenly in the middle of the night. I don't know what woke me up—perhaps a dream, although I couldn't remember it. But I had only one thought in my mind when I woke up—I was in terrible danger. I never should have gone with Charlotte. I'd become too comfortable, I'd fallen off my guard. In a weak moment I wanted to feel like a teenager again, carefree. But I should have known that was impossible. All I should have been worrying about was staying alive, staying out of trouble. And now, what if Herr Reymann discovered the truth? What if his wife did tell him eventually and he found out we'd been with an anti-Hitler gang? I'd be lucky to be sent back to Poland; they'd probably hang me right there, torturing me first to give up names. I couldn't sleep a wink the rest of the night. What was I to do? And I couldn't quite understand my panicked reaction. Didn't I *want* to die? Well, maybe I did but *only* on my own terms. I didn't want to be murdered.

When Charlotte came home from school the next day she motioned me to follow her to her room. She shut the door. "Close call," she said.

I nodded my head.

"You won't say anything?"

"Of course not," I said. "I'd be in awful trouble if they knew. But, Charlotte, your father would kill you if he found out."

"I'll be careful," she promised. "Georg met me after school and walked me part of the way home," she confided. "It was lucky we left when we did. Believe it or not, just as they were leaving, the gang heard noises in the forest and saw someone running. The boys caught up with him—it was a Jew who had managed to hide in Weimar but he'd been discovered. Where did he think he was going to hide?"

"What happened?" I asked.

"Oh, they dragged him to the police station, of course," Charlotte replied. "Still, I'm glad we weren't there."

"I don't understand," I said quietly. "I thought the Pirates hated Hitler."

"So?"

I stared at Charlotte. "Nothing." Of course, hating Hitler didn't mean they thought he was wrong about the Jews. Why should it?

But Charlotte wasn't more careful. She continued her nightly walks, where she met Georg. And I heard her sneaking out of the house again only three days later. All I could think about was what might happen to *me* if she were discovered. My part in that night would certainly come out. The danger felt real and immediate. I thought about nothing else for days until, finally, I realized that there was one way for me to avoid disaster. But my salvation meant betraying Charlotte. And Charlotte trusted me. But Charlotte didn't know I was a Jew. And had she known she wouldn't have spared me a thought as I was killed.

So one night, just after Charlotte went out for her walk, I asked Herr Reymann if I could speak privately to him. He looked a little surprised but told me to wait for him in his study. I stood awkwardly by the door, rehearsing in my mind what I was going to say.

He strode in and sat behind his desk. He was dressed in full Nazi uniform as he'd been to a meeting in Weimar that day. I started to feel a little light-headed.

"Please," he said, "sit down, Maria." He motioned to a chair. I actually made a move to leave but felt so dizzy that I sat down heavily in the chair, instead. He waited patiently.

"Herr Reymann," I began, my voice quivering slightly, "I would like to confide something to you. But I must ask you to promise me that what I say will remain confidential."

His eyebrows went up. "I cannot promise until I hear what you have to say," he replied.

I nodded mutely. It was too late to turn back. "Herr Reymann, the other night Frau Reymann caught Charlotte and me coming home late. Charlotte told her that we'd been to a party."

He paused, trying to hide any emotions but I could see he was upset. "Really? Go on."

I cleared my throat. "I have to tell you, it was the first time I'd gone with Charlotte. She has snuck out a number of times, at night."

His expression turned grim. "Go on."

"Yes. And, well, I feel that you need to know, she's gotten in with a rather bad crowd."

"How so?"

"They're one of those anti-Hitler groups. They are a large gang, and well . . . you see, Charlotte likes this one boy. Honestly, I know she doesn't agree with this gang, it's just this one boy. . . ." I rushed on. "I thought, well, if you could do something without letting her know, she'd lose interest in this group."

He got up from his chair and began to pace.

"She has deceived us."

"Yes, I know, but she's young."

"So are you. But even you can see . . ."

Even I. I knew what he meant. A Pole with some German blood, but an inferior Slav. Nevertheless, I didn't have time to be upset by his remarks. I had to follow the plan I'd set out for myself.

"The thing is, from what I can gather, this boy she likes isn't employed. None of the gang is. Please excuse me if I overstep my place by making a suggestion but if you could help this boy—get him work, maybe away from here—then she'd stop being with this gang, and a crisis could be averted."

He sat down again and stared at me. "My inclination would be to confront her. To punish her. How else will she learn?"

"I am her age," I said, my voice meek. "I know I am not her equal. But if I may suggest . . . ?"

"Yes, yes . . . what?"

"I think if you act in that way, first she will know I told you and will never trust me again. And then I won't be able to watch her for you. And also, she may become angry. She'll do something rash—run away, even."

He drummed his fingers on the desk and considered. "You took a risk admitting all this to me."

"I know," I admitted. "But I care about Charlotte and I can see she is out of her depth."

He got up. "What is the boy's name?"

"Georg Eberlein."

He reached out his hand and shook mine. "Thank you," he said. "This couldn't have been easy for you."

I forced myself to walk calmly to my room where I sank into my bed, trembling from head to foot. I had just betrayed Charlotte. At that moment, imagining how she would treat me if she knew I was Jewish, didn't help. I felt horrible, somehow dirty. And what if Herr Reymann went after the entire group? Had I given them all up to ensure my own safety? I felt sick. I lay down on the bed and when the boys called me to help with their homework I told them I was ill. About ten minutes later Frau Reymann came into the room.

"Why don't you stay in bed and rest tonight," she suggested. "That must have been very hard for you, Maria. But sometimes being a good friend means making a difficult choice. Thank you." And softly she closed the door.

A nervous laugh burst out of me. I clapped my hand over my mouth so they couldn't hear me.

But it was funny. If they only knew what was behind my noble behavior.

SIXTEEN

THREE DAYS LATER Charlotte came in after school, ran to her room, and burst out crying so loudly we could hear her from downstairs. Frau Reymann caught my eye and motioned me to go to her. I didn't want to. Her pain was a direct result of my actions and I had no doubt about why she was crying. But I had to continue to play the role of concerned little Polish servant girl. I knocked on her door.

"Go away!"

"Charlotte, it's me."

She opened the door for me, then threw herself down on her pink and white coverlet. "Georg is going away," she hiccupped.

"Oh, no," I managed to get out.

"All the way to Stuttgart," she sobbed. "He's been offered a very good job in a factory there."

"Well," I said, "he'll be back."

"No," she cried, "he won't. Because by next year he'll be called up and he'll have to fight. I'll never see him again!"

The image of Shmuel, tall, with his huge blue eyes gazing at me, hit me then with such force that my eyes filled with tears. Charlotte noticed.

"Oh, Maria," she said, throwing her arms around me, "what a good friend you are!" I patted her back and tried not to shrink away from her but it wasn't easy. I hated her. The Nazis had taken away my Shmuel. But I was fond of her, too; I was, I couldn't deny it. I didn't *want* to like her, though, so I made myself cold inside. I wouldn't let them wriggle their way inside of me. I'd *pretend* to be her friend, but never more than that.

And then I realized that my plan had succeeded admirably. Not only was I no longer in danger of being discovered, but Herr and Frau Reymann now owed me the deliverance of their daughter. I could relax—I'd be able to stay there indefinitely, secure in their gratitude.

We always think we know what the future will bring but we have no idea. We don't know what the next second will bring. And we're always surprised when it's different from what we expect, but why are we surprised? Our mistake is to expect *anything*. On the other hand, how can we not?

Little Christian was still giggling when we sat down for dinner that night. I had been playing house with him, dressing him up like a grown-up, and he looked very funny. Herr Reymann cleared his throat. He looked uncomfortable, and very serious.

"I'm afraid I have some bad news," he announced. "It can't be avoided, I'm afraid. There's been a general call for workers who can speak both Polish and German. Naturally, I had to submit Maria's name. Now they want her for a factory in

Berlin. It is filled with new Polish workers who can barely understand what is being asked of them."

I couldn't believe it. Just when I had a measure of security. I wondered if it had anything to do with what I'd told them. Maybe they were angry with me for sneaking out that night. Maybe they didn't want me there anymore. I knew that Berlin was being bombed, Charlotte had told me. I didn't want to go.

"But there *must* be workers there who can speak or understand German," I suggested. "It's hard to believe there isn't *someone.*"

"Yes, Vati," Charlotte protested, her eyes still red, "there must be someone. You can't take Maria away."

"Really, Heydrich," Frau Reymann remonstrated, "I can't believe this! We need Maria here. I won't let her go!"

What if I leaped up, right now, I thought, *and screamed, "I'm a Jew! I'm a Jew! You all want a Jew to stay here with you!"*

"It can't be helped," he answered. "I'm upset, too. But the factories have to produce and they desperately need translators." He turned to me. "You won't have to work on the machines. Maybe help in the kitchen, that sort of thing, when you aren't translating." He paused. "I'm sorry, my dear. We really would prefer it if you could stay on with us." He gave me a meaningful look. "Honestly there was no way I could prevent this."

He must have known what I was thinking. He seemed sincere, but I still didn't trust him.

Charlotte started to cry again. "Vati," she said,

"you, you, you're . . ." Of course she couldn't say anything disrespectful so she bit her cheek.

Christian also started to cry and he ran from the table. His mother threw down her napkin and followed him.

"When do I leave?"

"Tomorrow."

Anton and Tadeusz looked very upset but they could say nothing. After dinner they each gave me a little pep talk about keeping my wits about me and not getting in the way of any bombs. Impulsively I gave them each a kiss. They'd managed to make me feel just a little more human because they were victims, too.

I packed after dinner. Charlotte gave me a small suitcase along with lots of her old clothes. Although I was two years older than her we wore almost the same size.

I hardly slept that night. In the morning Charlotte came into my room first thing.

"Maria?"

"Yes."

"You will write me, won't you?"

"Of course I will."

"And if it's awful there, Vati will have you moved back here, I'm *sure* he will. I'll *make* him."

"I hope it'll be fine."

"But dangerous. The allies are bombing Berlin all the time now. How *could* Vati?"

"Charlotte," I reprimanded her, "remember your duty is always to the Fatherland first. Your father had no choice. He had to put Germany before his own family. You must respect him for that. Correct?"

She looked down, abashed. "Of course, you're right as always."

She sat on the bed, beside my suitcase.

"Can I tell you a secret, if you promise never to tell anyone?"

"Of course."

"Sometimes," she said, a small blush on her cheeks, "I imagine that we are really sisters. I pretend that both your parents are German and that you are an Aryan. If that were true, we would be as close as sisters."

She meant it. Her eyes were filled with tears.

I didn't know what to say in reply. So I patted her hand. "Study hard."

"I will."

I closed my suitcase. "I'm ready."

"Vati is waiting," she said. "He'll drive you to the train himself." And then she threw her arms around me and hugged me.

I got into the car beside Herr Reymann. He said little. Just before we reached the station, he spoke. "Maria, should you encounter any difficulties, please advise me. I meant what I said at dinner. This is in no way a punishment for your actions. I respect you for your decision, not an easy one. And I regret you must go to such a dangerous place but there seems to be no way to avoid it. Since our loss . . ."

I dared not ask what loss he was referring to

and he stopped himself as if it had just slipped out.

He settled me on the train and told me what streetcars I must take when I reached Berlin. The train pulled out.

Oh, Fanny, I thought, *I miss you so terribly. Charlotte wanted to be my sister. But I had the most perfect sister in the world, no matter how annoying she was. Stay alive, Fanny,* I thought, *please. Somehow.*

When the train pulled into Berlin I was awed by what a huge city it was. There was damage everywhere, though. The bombing was far worse than anything I had imagined. I got off the train and managed to find my way by streetcar to the factory. It was a large complex with numerous buildings surrounding the factory, no doubt for the foreign workers who were forced to work there. It was almost dark. The lights in the factory were still on, though. The foreman introduced himself as Herr Frank. He looked exhausted and cranky but not necessarily mean. In fact, he was very happy to see me.

"You'll sleep over in those barracks," he said, "with the other Polish women. They are terrible workers," he complained. "We must get production up. You will help with that. Tomorrow I'll explain what they are doing wrong. If they don't understand, they can ask you, and you'll tell me. It should help."

The air-raid sirens began to wail.

"Oh! There we go. We'll have to close the factory for the night now. Hurry along to your barracks."

The barracks didn't have any bomb shelters. When I walked in I saw twelve girls, some lying on their bunks and praying, some lying under their bunks. I was filled with conflicting emotions. I was terrified of being blown up by a bomb. On the other hand, they were British bombs. Or American bombs. They were fighting for us. And if I had to die, I would rather have died that way, because it meant that more people could be saved. The world could be saved. I took a deep breath and tried not to be afraid. I refused to let my old fears overtake me. I'd been through too much. Let the bombs hit. Let them bomb the Germans into submission.

I was determined to ask my fellow Poles what loss Herr Reymann was talking about. I could finally find out what was happening with the war. Strangely, although I was in terrible danger, my heart began to lift. Out there, in the country, it seemed that Germany was invincible. But if that were true the Allies couldn't have been so close. Perhaps there was hope.

SEVENTEEN

I MADE ONE FRIEND and one enemy almost immediately. Berthe took an immediate dislike to me, calling me "Little Miss Perfect" or "shrimp," whereas Renatta was thankful that I was there and could help them.

"These Germans," she muttered. "They expect us to work but we can't understand a word they say. What are we to do?"

The factory was part of the German war effort, producing bombs for 128-mm anti-aircraft guns. The workers had to cut these with great precision and grind them to the perfect tolerance or the part was unusable. I suspected that the Polish workers were making mistakes on purpose but I explained everything to them exactly as the foreman had instructed me to.

Berthe demanded that I tell him they wanted shorter work hours. I told her that she must be dreaming to ask for such a thing. She and the girls she had around her insisted, so I relayed their demands to him.

"You tell them," he said, "that they can be sent to our correction-through-work camp for workers who don't behave. I don't much think they'd enjoy themselves there. If anything, hours will increase. Especially after what just happened."

"A terrible loss for Germany," I replied, taking a stab at getting an answer to what was going on in the war.

"Our Führer told us that the Russians were our inferiors," the foreman said, voice low. "And yet, they defeat us at Stalingrad. Now at Kursk Salient they break the back of our panzers. And they are headed straight for Berlin! They are barbarians, those Russians. What will they do to us if they get here? You *must* convince those girls to work harder."

My heart was racing. The Germans on the run? The Russian "barbarians" on their way to Berlin? Had this man no idea what the Germans had been doing in countries like Poland?

I gave his message to the girls who seemed quite frightened at the idea of a work camp. Berthe grumbled, but even she realized that she was powerless to demand anything.

I was put to work in the kitchen when I was not translating, helping to dole out food, then cleaning up. One of the other workers was a sixteen-year-old called Ilse, who had been forced to quit school in order to help in the war effort. She was very shy and quiet. At first she barely spoke to me, looking at me as if, because I was Polish, I was a different species altogether. I made an effort to be friendly, though, and slowly, over a matter of weeks, she began to speak to me, but hesitantly, as if I might bite her.

One afternoon as we were clearing dishes she told me of vacations her family always took in the fall, by a beautiful lake.

I described the beauty of the area I came from, the old castle near the center of the city, the lakes and forests. She seemed stunned.

"But, you must be mistaken," she said. "Poland's a land of swamps. Nothing beautiful grows there."

"I've lived there all my life," I replied. "Why would I lie to you? Maybe someone else lied to you."

This upset her terribly and she avoided me for a while. But I didn't mind. I didn't need her because I finally had a friend, a real friend, not like Charlotte who was my master. Renatta and I spent all our time together after work. She was eighteen and had been forced to come to Germany. She was tall and a bit clumsy, all arms and legs, and she constantly made mistakes at the factory that everyone attributed to her being uncoordinated, but I knew that wasn't the case. She was very clever and could do anything; she simply chose not to help the German war effort. One tiny mistake and the part was scrap.

There were many boys in the factory, too; German boys as well as Polish, Belgian, Dutch. Everyone had to wear a letter that showed which country they came from. One of the Dutch boys, Jo, had gone sweet on Renatta. He was a university student, blond and blue-eyed. He could have been my brother.

With Renatta I felt like a girl again. She whispered secrets to me about her and Jo. We gossiped about the other girls. She even fussed about how she looked. And how I looked. She braided my hair in a French braid and put rouge on my cheeks. She teased me when some of the Polish boys flirted with me. She teased me even more when the German boys flirted with me. One in particular, Otto, was relentless in his attentions. He had been wounded in battle and had hurt his foot,so he'd been sent to work in the factory. One day he gave me an aluminum ring made out of the material in the factory.

In a way, I was glad to be there rather than with the Reymanns, even though it was far more dangerous in Berlin. Because after months of being with people, but alone, I'd forgotten how wonderful it was to be with a friend, to have a friend. Renatta even protected me against Berthe's nasty comments and kept her away from me.

One night Renatta confided to me that she and Jo were going to the movies and asked me to join them.

"But are we allowed?" I asked.

"Of course not!" Renatta answered. "But we take off our *P*s and go anyway. Even if we get caught they can't really punish us. They need us now, Maria. They're in trouble." She grinned.

"All right!" I agreed. Shmuel wouldn't recognize me, I thought. Where was the helpless little girl he once knew?

As we traveled through the city we could see bombed-out buildings and smoldering ruins everywhere. It was unsettling because I hated to see that kind of destruction and yet Berlin was the enemy, so I had to be glad.

Spring Melody was a romantic comedy, a silly little movie with no reference to the war at all, no intimation that death and destruction hovered around us. Renatta giggled at its foolishness and her silliness infected me. We ate candy and laughed and I managed to thoroughly enjoy myself.

I was still in such good humor the next day at work that at first I didn't notice something was wrong with Ilse. But as she cleaned the tables her hands shook so hard she could barely hold the cloth, and tears sprang to her eyes. I pulled her over to a chair and sat down beside her. "What is it?" I asked.

"My father," she said to me, bursting into sobs. "He's been executed by the Gestapo."

"Oh, I'm so sorry," I exclaimed, and I meant it. Perhaps she could feel that I was sincere because suddenly she was telling me everything. "He is, he was a minister. He never did anything wrong. He was denounced by our neighbors for listening to the BBC on the radio. That's not a crime, surely it's not a death crime. He was sent to the people's court and they guillotined him. And then, today, Mother received this in the mail." She pulled it out and showed it to me:

BOARD PER DAY	1.50
TRANSPORT TO BRANDENBURG PRISON	12.90
EXECUTION OF SENTENCE	158.18
FEE FOR DEATH SENTENCE	300.00
POSTAGE	1.84
POSTAGE FOR STATEMENT COST	.42
TOTAL RM	474.84

"One hundred and fifty-eight reichsmarks to kill

him. I have to take it in to the Gestapo head-
quarters and pay it today or they'll take everything
we own. People are disappearing all the time.
The Gestapo is everywhere. The worse the war
news gets the worse they get. I don't understand.
We've always been good Germans. We've always
obeyed."

"Perhaps that's where you went wrong. It isn't
right to obey blindly. Or to obey those who don't
deserve your trust."

"But, we love our Führer," she said.

"Do you? Still?"

"No!" she exploded. "I hate him. And I hate the
Gestapo."

"Shsh," I cautioned her, "or you'll end up like
your father. Go and pay the bill. I'll finish up
here."

She left, and I had to admit to myself that I was
glad she'd turned against Hitler even if it had
taken her father's death to make her do it. After
all, how many Jewish fathers had had to die
because of him? On the other hand, I was sorry
for her. And for her father, but I felt less pity for
him. After all, you'd think the ministers would
have been the first to oppose Hitler. Instead, most
had backed him. Charlotte had explained to me
how important the church had been in the Third
Reich. Well, if he was going to die, he would have
been better off fighting evil. At least then, his
death would have meant something.

It started to get cool, although November in

Berlin was mild compared to Zloczow. One night, after it turned cloudy and drizzly, Renatta suggested another movie—everyone assumed that the bombers wouldn't come, as they liked clear weather so they could see their targets.

We got off the streetcar and right in front of us was a huge poster. I had learned since arriving in Berlin that posters were a large part of the propaganda campaign the Nazis ran constantly. That particular one depicted a worker, except in place of his head, was a goose's head. Under that image, large print declared: SHAME ON YOU, BIG MOUTH —THE ENEMY IS LISTENING—SILENCE IS YOUR DUTY!

But someone had scratched out the word "enemy" and put SS instead. Renatta laughed.

"Jo told me this joke," she said. "'Two Berliners meet in the street. One complains bitterly, 'The news is terrible. If this goes on, we're sure to lose the war.'

"'Yes, I know,' says the other, 'but *when*?'"

As we sat and waited for the picture to start, I told her about Shmuel. I had to change his name, of course—I called him Wolf. I told her how smart he was, how good looking, how we were cousins but we really weren't. I'd have given anything to share my big secret with her. But only last week a girl was turned in by her boyfriend after she had confessed to him she was Jewish. I trusted people, but only to a point.

"Will you invite me to your wedding?" Renatta said.

I was about to answer when the air-raid siren wailed.

"Oh, no," Renatta moaned, "I was looking forward to the movie!"

EIGHTEEN

"WE'D BETTER FOLLOW EVERYONE to the nearest shelter," I suggested. "At least we won't have to sit in our barracks, completely unprotected, tonight."

We hurried along with the rest of the crowd and followed them into a public shelter. It was crowded with moviegoers and people who had been eating in the restaurant next door. We could hear the airplanes and we could hear the flak and then we heard the first explosions, like distant thunder. They got closer and closer, the way a storm does, until the bombs were falling all around us, shaking the shelter in an unending deluge. The Allies must have been trying to destroy the entire city. No one spoke. Occasionally someone gasped in fear. A child sobbed quietly. And then, suddenly, a young boy of maybe ten started to scream, "Let me out, let me out!" His mother tried to hang on to him but he slipped past her and got all the way to the door, where we were standing. Renatta, big and strong as she was, lifted him like he was a little doll.

Renatta couldn't speak German well—if she opened her mouth everyone would know she was a

Pole and they'd throw us out—so I spoke for her.

"You don't want to go out there," I said while she calmly held him in the air.

"Yes I do, let me go, let me go."

"It's much more dangerous out there," I assured him as he wriggled and kicked.

"I don't care!"

His mother finally struggled through the mass of people.

"Thank you," she gasped. "I couldn't keep hold of him. Thank you."

"She'll hold you all night," I warned the boy, "if you won't listen to your mother."

His struggles grew weaker and then he started to cry. He held his arms out to his mother who grasped him. He wrapped his arms around her neck and sobbed.

Bomb after bomb crashed around us. The air pressure changed as the bombs exploded. Beside me a man murmured his prayers. Another declared, "This is the worst. My God, my whole family is at home. How will anyone survive?"

Finally we could hear the destruction moving to a different part of the city, as a storm moves on. But the shelter began to fill with smoke. We had to get out. Renatta and I got caught behind the door and the crush of people pushing out the door. I couldn't breathe. I started to choke and gag. It was a horrible feeling. And suddenly a picture of Moishe choking filled me and I wondered if I shouldn't die like he did. Why should I live and he die? The thought, hitting me like that, froze me to the spot. Renatta grabbed me by the wrist and pulled me, using her height and strength to push a path through the crowd, which had now turned into a mob trying to get out of the small door. Renatta dragged me through, and up the stairs. For a split second at the shelter opening, we stopped, the scene before us so incomprehensible. The movie theater had vanished; so had the restaurant. Only heaps of rubble remained where they'd stood. But worse than that, everything was on fire, not only any buildings left standing but trees, bushes, flowers, even the grass on the street was on fire. There was smoke everywhere.

We were pushed from behind and forced to move.

"Where do we go?" I yelled. The noise of the fire and people screaming was very loud.

"I don't know," she shouted back. "Let's try to find shelter. Anywhere still standing."

And then right behind us a bomb exploded, lifting bodies into the air. Renatta and I were thrown forward onto the hot cement. Something landed on my arm—it was a hand, a hand with a wedding ring on it. I screamed. And then everything went black.

I woke up choking, Renatta hovering over me. "Are you all right? Were you hit?"

"I'm . . . I'm, I must have fainted. I'm sorry." Then I remembered. "Where is it? Where is it?" I started to flail around.

"Don't worry, it's gone," she answered.

She lifted me onto my feet. "Come on! We have to get out of here. Our enemies haven't killed us yet. I'm not going to let our friends do it for them. That must have been a time bomb back there. Remember that little boy and his mother . . . both killed." She pointed back to a mass of bodies. "Let's go!"

We stumbled forward for a couple blocks, into an area where buildings were still standing, but all of them were burning. I heard a cry for help coming from one of the houses we were passing. I stopped.

Renatta grabbed my wrist and pulled me forward. "We can't help anyone," she shouted. Fire raged around us; pieces of buildings fell on either side. The smoke was so thick I could barely see her. "Why should we help *them*?"

"We *have* to help," I shouted back. "There's no one else around. And it sounds like children. It's not their fault." I twisted my wrist and slipped out of her grasp, then ran toward the screams. It was girls voices, young and terrified. The upper half of the house was burning but the lower half seemed all right. Gingerly I touched the doorknob. It was so hot I couldn't turn it. I pulled my sweater over my hand and turned. Renatta stood in the street, calling my name, "Maria, Maria, don't!"

The hallway was filled with smoke but at least it wasn't on fire. The voices were coming from the basement. An open door showed stairs leading down. I put my sweater over my nose and mouth and cautiously stepped down the stairs. The voices were louder now, just behind the door. I tried to open the door but it wouldn't move. I knocked hard.

"Hello? Who's there?"

"Help! Help! We're trapped. The lock is jammed, we can't open the door." I tried but I couldn't either. Renatta appeared beside me. "What is it?"

"I don't know. The heat must've melted the lock. The door won't open."

Renatta lifted her leg and with all her might kicked at the doorknob. At first nothing happened but after a few forceful kicks the doorjamb gave way and the door opened. Two identical twins stood by the door on the other side. They were around twelve or thirteen, very pretty, blond hair braided with blue ribbons.

"Where are your parents?" I asked.

"Father is at the war," one said. "Mother wasn't home from work yet. It's our birthday. She was going to take us out when . . ."

There was a terrible crash. Renatta whirled around.

"Damn," she said.

"What?"

"The fire's spread. We're cut off. Look."

Sure enough, the staircase was on fire.

"Does this house connect with the others on the street?" Renatta asked the twins. But she spoke in Polish and they didn't understand. Quickly, I translated.

One began to cry. "Yes it does," she answered. "Will we die? Will we burn to death?"

"Stop," Renatta ordered in broken German. "Fear is no good. We'll figure out a way."

The cellar was filling up with dense smoke. I noticed a washtub and hustled the girls over to it.

"Take off your sweaters," I said, "and soak them in water." I did the same. "Renatta," I called, "give me your sweater." She was tapping on the walls. She handed me her sweater.

"Tools?" she asked the girls.

"Yes," they answered, "there."

Renatta found a hammer. I gave her the sweater back, wet. She put it on, then began to whack at the wall with all her strength. "Come, help me," she called. We each found something; I used an old chair leg and we hit the wall as hard as we could. Thankfully the wall was very thin and we managed to gouge a hole in it. We pushed the girls through, then we scrambled through ourselves.

We were in another cellar. There was an entire family in that one, an old woman, a mother, three children, a father. They, too, were trapped, the cellar filling with smoke. Since we had more people we were able to open a hole in the wall faster. And that time the hole led us to the street.

We gasped for air but the smoke was as bad outside as it was inside. The father yelled, "We must get to a shelter. Look at this fire. If it's like this all over the city there'll be a firestorm. I can feel it; the wind is picking up. The heat will make the wind something fierce."

It already was—the hot wind seared my face, and

the noise of the fire crackled and sizzled so loudly we could barely hear one another speak.

This time Renatta grabbed my arm and pulled me with all the force she had. I didn't resist. We staggered along, our wet sweaters over our noses, until we finally saw a street that wasn't completely on fire. There was a pub that was open and we scurried in. It was jammed with people. Renatta pulled me over to a corner and we crouched down out of the crush.

I tried to catch my breath. So did she.

"Think we're winning?" she said with a wink.

For a moment I didn't know what she meant.

"The war, stupid," she said, grinning. "The war."

NINETEEN

WE STAYED IN THAT PUB for hours. Because it hadn't been damaged by fire it had been taken over by The Women's League and the NSU, the Nazi Welfare Service. They served coffee—*real* coffee, not the fake kind people had been drinking all through the war—and Leberwurst sandwiches. Actually, we always used to drink tea at home and I'd never developed a taste for coffee but Renatta was thrilled. I sipped it, just for the liquid, and I *did* eat. People somehow heard about the pub and they streamed in all night, many lugging suitcases filled with the only possessions they had left. Most seemed in a state of shock.

By around three A.M. it was pouring rain, but even the rain didn't stop the fires. Outside, a tree lay across the road, and the wind flung window frames, tiles from the roofs, eaves, and bits of metal and glass, through the air. Renatta and I had tried to venture out earlier but we had quickly given up. Instead we huddled into a corner and despite the noise and commotion fell asleep, leaning on each other.

We were awakened by a huge crash just outside

the window. Something outside had collapsed. It had to be morning although the light was so dim from all the smoke it was hard to tell. We forced ourselves to go out realizing that we had to get back to the factory. It was a grim scene, but not as bad as the night before. The wind had abated at least. Smoldering ruins, craters the size of houses, mounds of rubble and glass were everywhere. Work crews were already digging in the rubble trying to find survivors.

"What do you think of your precious Hitler now?" Renatta muttered, viewing the destruction.

"They probably still love him," I answered. "Do you know that Charlotte told me that *Poland* had started the war? And she believes it! Everyone believes it."

Renatta snorted in disgust. "I don't think Hitler will be a big favorite for much longer."

We held hands as we walked through the ruins. Renatta managed to flag down a truck and get us a ride to quite near the factory. Except there was no factory. And out of all the large and small barracks only one, somehow, was left standing.

"Jo!" Renatta cried.

She started to run. I ran after her. We reached the men's barracks, all of which had been destroyed. About fifty men were sitting around, looking dazed but unhurt. Jo wasn't one of them. Renatta moved from person to person asking about him until she found a friend.

"It was an inferno," the friend said. "We were all

caught in it. Jo isn't dead. He's burned, though. They took him to the hospital."

"They had no protection here." Renatta said, between gritted teeth.

"But they took him to the hospital. They're taking care of him at least," I said, wishing the Germans had treated my family so well.

"Yes, and if it weren't for them he wouldn't be here in the first place would he?" she spat out. "I hate them!" She turned to me. "I have to go see him."

"Maria!" It was the foreman, Herr Frank, calling me. "You're alive! When we couldn't find you, we thought you were one of the dead."

He didn't even ask me where I'd been.

"The workers will be sent to another factory; we just don't know where yet," he said. "Our downtown office has been spared and we have other factories. Still, it could be days, even weeks, before everything is organized." And then he wandered off, muttering to himself.

I spent the day with Renatta going from hospital to hospital, searching for Jo. Some streetcars were running, as were some trains, but mainly we walked. Finally, at the third hospital, we found him. He was in a bed in the hallway, as all the beds in the hospital were full. The doctors and nurses worked frantically, dealing with burns, mutilations, serious cuts from glass, crushed bones—all the injuries a fire and bombing like that could cause. No one would talk to us to tell us how he was, and he couldn't speak—he seemed drugged. His arms were bandaged, as was his chest.

"They must have given him something strong for the pain," I said to Renatta in a low voice. "But he's alive. And look, his face is hardly burned, his legs are all right. . . . I think he'll be fine!'

"If he doesn't get an infection and die," she murmured. She shook her head as she stared at him. "We won't survive here, Maria. We have to get out of Berlin. Why should we die here? We don't live here. We don't need to be here."

"Then let's go somewhere else," I suggested.

She looked at me.

"You're right. No one will stop us. No one will notice. We'll leave as soon as Jo can travel."

We stayed and watched him. Finally he opened his eyes. He was in too much pain to smile, but I could tell that he recognized Renatta and his eyes spoke volumes about how he felt about her.

Just then, the air-raid sirens started again.

"Don't worry," she assured Jo, "I won't leave you."

He tried to shake his head. He tried to speak, but his voice wouldn't work. He must've inhaled a lot of smoke during the bombing.

"Renatta, he wants us to go to the basement," I said. "He's worried about you."

He nodded his head ever so slightly. "Come on," I urged, pulling at her, "he'll just worry if we're here."

"I don't want to leave him!" she declared.

"Renatta!" It was my turn to pull her away. "You can't help him this way."

I managed to get her down to the basement. The electricity was still out so we sat in darkness with at least a hundred others. And then we heard the bombs again. It sounded just like the night before. Of course, the city had to be an easy target, still burning brightly. We tried to take our minds off the danger by making plans.

"We could go to another city, find another factory to work in," she whispered.

"I think we should," I agreed. And then I realized something quite wonderful. I didn't want to die any more. That is, I didn't feel like killing myself. And I hadn't had those thoughts for quite a long time. There I was making plans, planning a way to stay alive! Impulsively I grabbed Renatta's hand.

"What a good friend you are," I said fervently.

"Well, someone had to take pity on you."

"What do you mean?"

"When you arrived. You looked so miserable. I've never seen such a forlorn face."

"So you took *pity* on me. I'm insulted."

"Pity," she repeated, grinning. "And you're lucky I did. Otherwise *Berthe* might have got you."

I shuddered. And I grinned back. "I guess pity's not so bad."

We could hear the planes overhead, the flak, the counterattack.

A bomb exploded very near us. We clutched each other's hands. "That's one more for us," she whispered.

When the raid was finally over we went back

upstairs to see Jo, but he was still too drugged to talk. We realized that we had nowhere to sleep. The factory barracks, after all, were bombed out.

"If we go back I'm sure Herr Frank will send us to a different factory," Renatta said.

"Yes, and then we may be stuck. We could stay here," I suggested. "No one will notice us. We could sleep in the shelters, eat hospital food, and wait for Jo to get better."

Jo got better much quicker than we expected. His burns were really not severe and within a week he was strong enough to travel. We decided to go back to Weimar, to the employment office. They did know me there. Maybe, just maybe they'd let all of us stay with the Reymanns again. I could stand it if I had Renatta with me, a real friend, someone I could talk to and confide in. The three of us managed to get ourselves on a train that took two days to get to Weimar. When we got off we saw that Weimar, too, had been bombed.

"You again!" The employment officer looked at me with surprise. "Now what?"

"Our factory was bombed out in Berlin," I explained. "So I've come back here. I was wondering if Herr Reymann still needs help. . . ."

"And these two?"

"*Very* good workers," I assured him. "If they could be with me?"

"Well," he paused, "we really don't need help on the farms now with winter coming. But we have a slaughterhouse that needs workers. The three of you could share a small flat near there."

We looked at each other. As long as I wasn't separated from Renatta I didn't mind. I nodded my head. They agreed as well.

"That's settled, then," he said. "You can go over there right away. The telephones still aren't working since the last raid, so I'll write out a note for the foreman." He looked at me. "I'm sure the Reymanns would like it if you went out to visit."

Visit my Nazi friends. Why not?

"Of course," I said, "as soon as I can I'll go out there."

The three of us went to report to our new jobs.

TWENTY

I WAS WASHING OUT intestines when Herr Reymann came into the factory.

"Hello, Maria."

"Hello, Herr Reymann. What a surprise."

"The employment officer informed me of your return."

I motioned to Renatta to cover for me for a moment.

"I would request that you join our family for dinner tonight," he said. "Charlotte very much wants to see you. In fact, we would like you to come and work for us again." He paused. "I never should have let you leave."

He looked sincere; like he really meant it.

"But my friends . . ."

"Ah, you have made some friends. Good. Good for you. Well, of course, whenever you have time you may visit them in town. Or they are welcome to come out to the farm. You can ride to town with me if you like."

"I had asked to go to your farm," I said, "but the employment officer told me that there was too little work."

He grimaced. "Frau Reymann badly needs help right now. I can't explain here. Please. Will you come?"

He really needn't have asked me so politely. I was sure that the employment office would have jumped if he had simply snapped his fingers and they would have ordered me to go to his farm. Still, it was nice to be treated as if I weren't a slave. I decided to keep up the pretense.

"Of course I will come," I agreed. "Now?"

"Yes, now. I'll wait while you wash up."

I hurried over to Renatta. "That is the Herr Reymann I told you about. I'm sorry but I have to go with him."

"Have to?" she asked.

"Don't really have a choice, do I? I'll go to our flat and collect my things. And I'll come back to visit first chance I get."

Actually, I was really a third wheel in that flat with her and Jo and we all knew it. Of course I could have made a fuss but I was probably better off out of their way. And I *didn't* want to go back to living in a barracks. Also, although it was strange to admit it, I had missed the family. I'd missed the children, even though I was so lonely and miserable there. Now that I had a real friend only a few miles away, I reasoned I wouldn't feel as lonely this time. I was surprised by my own feelings at that moment—very surprised.

I washed up, and then Herr Reymann took me to get my clothes. Our flat was quite decent. Our job had entailed pushing water from a hose through the intestine which often resulted in excess fat. The factory foreman had allowed Renatta and me to collect the fat that came out of the intestines when we'd cleaned them. We'd sold the fat to people who wanted it for cooking and we'd bought clothes, food, even treats for ourselves. It had made me feel quite rich.

Herr Reymann seemed rather surprised when he saw our flat. I'm sure he assumed that all Poles were slovenly, dirty, and lived in pigsties. In the car he was quiet. I wanted to ask him why Frau Reymann needed me but I felt quite tongue-tied.

When we got out of the car the first thing I saw was Charlotte, standing outside waiting for us. It was January, and there was a slight dusting of snow on the ground but it was a fairly mild day. Still, I had to wonder how long she'd been standing outside like that. She shrieked when she saw me, ran to me, and threw her arms around me. Part of me felt cold, felt nothing. After all, I was still only a servant, a stupid Pole, worse if she only knew the truth, so why should I have felt anything for her? But another part of me melted, a part of my heart, because I could feel that she loved me.

"Keep love in your heart, Marisa, not hate!" I heard Shmuel again. Always Shmuel. Lecturing me forever.

Christian burst out the door and was ready to throw himself at me too, but then remembered that he was a big boy of almost twelve. He shook my hand solemnly.

Frau Reymann greeted me at the door taking both my hands in hers. "Maria, my dear, I'm so glad you are safe. We all hoped for your safety when we heard of the terrible raids on Berlin. You must have such stories to tell. Come in. Come in."

"Where's Hans?" I asked.

Her eyes immediately filled with tears.

"But didn't Herr Reymann tell you?"

"No."

"Come with me."

She led me to Hans' room. He lay propped up in bed and he smiled as soon as he saw me. He was tucked under the covers.

"Hello Hans," I said, coming in. "Aren't you well?"

"He can't move," Charlotte explained. "He's paralyzed from his shoulders down."

"But how?" I moved over to him and put a hand on his forehead. A tear trickled down his face. Frau Reymann hurried to dry it for him.

"He enlisted without telling us," his mother said. "He took a bullet in his spine."

"But he's too young."

"They'll take them at any age now—officially they must be fourteen, but they don't check," she said, her voice neutral as she tried to keep the emotion out of it.

I knelt by his bed. "It's all right, Hans," I assured him, "I'm here now. I'll help your mother and we'll take good care of you."

"His wheelchair arrives tomorrow," Herr Reymann said. "It took some doing to get him one."

"Can you speak Hans?" I asked.

"Yes," he replied, his voice weak.

"You can speak, and you can swallow," I said. "That's good! When your wheelchair comes and you can get out of bed you'll feel better."

He closed his eyes.

"He's tired now," murmured Frau Reymann. "Best let him rest."

We went out into the living room. "You see," said Herr Reymann, "we really do need your help."

"I'm so sorry," I said. And I was. And yet how could I be? Wasn't that the same child who had played Jews Out when I first arrived? Who couldn't wait to go fight and kill Poles and Jews? How could I feel sorry for him and his family? It was so confusing I felt light-headed.

"Sit down dear," Frau Reymann said. "You've turned absolutely white. What a shock we've given you." She ran and got me a glass of water. "Why don't you go unpack. You'll have your old room back. And then we'll have dinner."

And so, I was back with my "family," a twisted version of my real family, almost like the negatives in a picture. But in some way I could not explain I was connected to them and I felt for them. I unpacked my clothes and lay down on the bed to rest for a moment. . . .

"Papa!"

"Marisa."

"Papa, I haven't seen you in so long."

"Marisa, what did I tell you the last time we spoke?"

"That all I need is in the Torah. That I should go to the Torah if I need help."

"That's right."

"But Papa, I can't remember the Torah anymore! I can't even remember how to speak Yiddish. Sometimes I try to practice at night, but the words come out German. I've *completely* forgotten. I can't remember any Hebrew prayers. Only the Shehecheyanu. I'm not a Jew anymore, am I, Papa?"

"Would the Nazis say that, Marisa?"

"No, they'd say I'm a Jew no matter what I remember or don't remember."

"For once, I agree with them. You are a Jew. What did Shmuel tell you? Keep love in your heart? Love is God. And God can exist only if you let Him into your heart. You remember the Shema, don't you? Of course you do. 'Shema Israel, Adonai Eloheinu, Adonai Ekhad. Hear, O Israel: the Lord Our God, the Lord is One.' That's all you have to remember. What does it mean, my little scholar?"

"'One' refers to all of us, we are all part of God."

"That's right little one. Even those Nazis you are living with. Doesn't each of them have a spark of the divine? Doesn't each of them have a soul? That is what you must see when you see them, not the rest. Don't be confused. It's simple."

"Papa! It's simple when you say it like that. But you'd have to be a saint not to hate them for what they are."

"Not a saint. Hate won't help you, Marisa little

darling. Hate won't help you. Now say it over so you remember: 'Shema Israel, Adonai . . .'"

"Maria! Maria. You've been crying out in your sleep."

It was Charlotte. "You were muttering some strange language, Maria."

I sat up in bed. My heart pounded, the blood rushed to my cheeks. I'd been discovered.

"What were you talking?" she asked.

She didn't know. She didn't recognize Hebrew.

"Russian!" I said. "You know the Russians invaded our town before the Germans. I learned to speak it fluently."

"You're amazing. Wait till I tell Father this."

"No!"

"You don't want me to tell?"

"Who knows, maybe there will be a job for a Russian translator and I'll be sent away again."

"You're right," she said. "I hadn't thought of that. Don't worry, I won't say a word. I just came to tell you how happy I am you're home with us. I've missed you terribly. Maria," she continued, "are you a *little* fond of me then? *Almost* like I could be your sister?" She sounded so wistful.

"But I'm just your servant," I snapped at her, wishing Papa hadn't spoken to me in the dream.

She whispered, "I know. And that makes me so confused. Because I love you like a sister, Maria, not like a servant. I wouldn't even mind if you pulled my hair or yelled at me because I'm annoying you. Because that's what sisters do. I know I shouldn't say this but they must have been wrong about the Poles. I've learned to like Anton and Tadeusz, too. They aren't stupid and neither are you. And I think, well, I have to wonder, could the Nazi Party be wrong, what they are making us girls do? All my friends are going with boys, to have babies for the Reich. But I'm frightened. I don't want to. The boys grab me and grope at me; I hate them all. I run away. And they say they'll report me if I don't. . . ." She started to cry. "Father and Mother will want me to do my duty. But I can't. You're the only one I can tell." Her tears turned to sobs.

Her crying pierced my heart. If only she knew how I'd betrayed her to save myself. I wanted to ask her about Georg but I couldn't bring myself to.

Gingerly I put my arms around her, feeling almost like I was embracing a land mine. She dropped her head on my shoulder and gasped, "You'll help me, won't you, Maria? Please. I can't go on like this."

I stroked her hair and tried to soothe her. And the huge hunk of ice in my heart started to melt away, which scared me.

"We're all scared," I said. Suddenly, out of nowhere, although I thought I'd forgotten all my Torah, I remembered a line from Ezekiel: "'I will take away the stony heart . . . and I will give you a heart of flesh.'"

And then I remembered something Papa used to say to me, when I had trouble at school with Poles who hated Jews. "It is better for my enemy to see good in me than for me to see evil in him."

Thank you, Papa, I said silently. *Thank you.*

And to Charlotte I said, "Don't worry. We'll figure something out. You aren't alone anymore."

Epilogue

THE WAR ENDED. A thousand times after Germany was defeated I opened my mouth to tell the Reymanns that I was Jewish. But I couldn't. I stayed on the farm with them—they wanted me to stay forever. But one day, without telling anyone on the farm, I went to the American in charge of Weimar and told him who I was. He was Jewish. An American Jew. *At least there were American Jews still alive,* I thought, *even though all of us in Europe have surely been killed.* He told me to go to a displaced persons camp run by the United Nations. He suggested that I return to Poland but I was afraid of what I'd find. No one left alive. No one but me.

I decided that if I was going to leave I should leave quickly. The Reymanns asked me over and over to stay. I told them that I must return to my family who loved me and needed to see me. What would they think when they wrote to my "address" in Poland and no one answered? Would they begin to suspect, or would they just assume that I had forgotten them?

I said a tearful good-bye. Charlotte clung to me. "I love you Maria," she cried. "Don't forget me."

"I won't," I said, "I promise I won't."

I had said good-bye to Renatta and Jo months ago. The minute the Americans arrived they had arranged to go home. After things had calmed down and Renatta had seen her family, she was planning to go to Holland. I promised to write as soon as I knew where I'd be. I told them both that I was a Jew at our last meeting.

"You could have trusted me," Renatta had said. "I would *never* have betrayed you. We hid a Jewish family for as long as we could when the Germans came."

"I couldn't trust anyone that much," I said. "I'm sorry. I hope you understand."

She looked hurt and sad, but she said we'd always be best friends. Even when I was at the Reymanns we saw each other often—she, in fact, became a great favorite of the children, too.

The two Polish workers, Anton and Tadeusz, left right away, also. They couldn't understand why I'd wanted to stay. They didn't know that I had no home left, nothing to return to. But maybe, just maybe, Fanny or Yehuda or Shmuel were still alive. I had stayed at the Reymanns so long because the truth was, I was afraid that if I discovered I really was all alone, I wouldn't have the strength to carry on.

Still, when I said my good-byes I felt awful. Charlotte *had* become like my little sister, I had taken care of Hans for so long, Christian doted on me. . . . How could I have become attached to them like this? And yet, how could I not?

I cried as Herr Reymann drove me to the train. He shook my hand and thanked me for being so wonderful to his family.

"Herr Reymann," I said, "I'm . . . I'm . . ."

"Yes?"

"I'm not what you think."

"What do you mean?"

"Nothing. Nothing." And I hurried to the train and waved good-bye.

At the DP camp I was given two blankets and some food, but I couldn't find anywhere to sleep. All the beds were taken. I asked in barrack after barrack if there was room. A woman said to me, "Soon, when the Jews leave, there'll be more room."

"Jews? What Jews?"

"The Jews in the DP camp across the way."

"There are Jews?"

"Yes."

"But I thought I was the only one. Perhaps a few left. But enough to make an entire camp?"

"Yes. And they have lists of Jews that are in other camps. The ones who lived."

I started to run. It couldn't be true, could it? No one could have survived. I stopped dead when I reached the camp. It was huge, enough to house hundreds, maybe even thousands. Desperately I asked directions until I reached the main office. A young man sat at a desk covered with papers.

"Is it true?" I was gasping for breath. "You have lists of those who are alive?"

"We have lists of those who are dead and lists

of the living, too. Which would you like to see first?"

"The living."

I sat down, hands trembling, and started to read. There were lots of names. Beside each name was the name of the DP camp the person was living in.

"You must register," the person at the desk said. "Someone could be looking for *you.*"

My hands were shaking so hard, I couldn't see the names properly. But then . . . Shmuel Ginsberg.

"Where, where is this . . ." I asked.

"Why, it's a camp not far from here, right in Germany."

Tears started to pour from my eyes.

"Hey. You're soaking that page. Others need to use it."

He must have come in as a foreign worker. Somehow he had fooled them all.

"Can I get there?"

"There's a convoy leaving in a few days. You can go on it."

What of Fanny? Yehuda? Their names were not on the lists. So I went over the lists of the dead. But there were so many. So many. I got to the Gs. Ginsberg. And there they were: Yitzhak Ginsberg— killed by the Ukrainian death squads. Sarah Ginsberg, Moishe Ginsberg, Rachel Ginsberg— killed in roundup. And then I read my cousins' names, my friends' names, name after name. . . . But Yehuda and Fanny were not listed. So there was hope. Perhaps they survived.

I survived. Protected by the Nazis that killed my family. Could I ever forgive myself?

Again I heard Shmuel's voice. And I remembered the Psalms we recited while hiding in Poland.

"Happy is the man who has not followed the counsel of the wicked . . . He is like a tree planted beside streams of water . . . and whatever it produces thrives."

I will be a scholar, Papa, I vowed. *I will document these times. I will tell this story. I will probably never understand how it could have happened. But I will try.*

And so, while waiting for my transportation to Shmuel's camp, I have tried to remember it all. To preserve it, no matter how much I would like to forget. A scholar cannot forget. A scholar has a duty. But I also will never forget the most important lesson I have learned: My scholarship must never take second place to my heart, because only there does God truly reside.

CAROL MATAS is the author of more than two dozen bestselling books for children and young adults, and is best known for her historical novels, including *Daniel's Story, After the War, Greater than Angels, Sworn Enemies, Lisa, Jesper* and *Rebecca*. She also writes contemporary fiction, as well as fantasy novels with co-author Perry Nodelman.

Carol's books have won many honors, including two Governor General's Award nominations, the Silver Birch Award, the Jewish Book Prize and the Red Maple Award. She lives in Winnipeg, Manitoba.